The Palm Beach Palace

And Other Stories

Estelle Craig

authorHOUSE®

AuthorHouse™
1663 Liberty Drive
Bloomington, IN 47403
www.authorhouse.com
Phone: 1 (800) 839-8640

Published by AuthorHouse 06/08/2018

ISBN: 978-1-5462-4309-0 (sc)
ISBN: 978-1-5462-4308-3 (e)

Print information available on the last page.

This book is printed on acid-free paper.

Contents

Chapter 1 A New Start for Leslie......................1

Chapter 2 Table for Six 8

Chapter 3 Breakfast Friends........................... 16

Chapter 4 A Buzz in the Palace 21

Chapter 5 Drama Club 30

Chapter 6 Mall Excursion 38

Chapter 7 Poolside Conversation 44

Chapter 8 A Diamond in the Rough 54

Chapter 9 Gary Makes a Plan 62

Chapter 10 Girl Talk 72

Chapter 11 Another New Beginning 81

Claudette, the Hairdresser...............................85

The Taxi Driver..93

"Build Me A Pyramid!" 107

Soul Mates...123

Dedicated to my three brilliant crown jewels
Sheri, Collin and Robin

Credits:
Cover Photo: Robin Melanie Craig
Editing: Sheri Ruttle and Angela Shaw

CHAPTER ONE

A New Start for Leslie

When Leslie Harper decided to move into the Palm Beach Palace, she had no idea how this would affect the rest of her life. The Palm Beach Palace was a residence for seniors. Although Leslie was approaching her 75th birthday, she felt more like 60 and looked it. She was slim, took pride in her figure, and stood 5 foot, 7 inches in heels. Her chestnut colored hair was nearly shoulder length. Her light brown eyes sparkled with excitement as she reached the door of the Palm Beach Palace.

She had passed by several times, but had never been inside. It wasn't until her husband, Bruce, suffered from a heart attack and died, however, that she began to seriously contemplate a change of residence. The house that she and her husband had shared for so many years started to feel rather lonely to Leslie.

Their marriage had been good, but not overly exciting. Bruce was a creature of habit; he liked coming home and having his dinner at 6:30 p.m. every night. He never really wanted to go out. He liked to stretch out each night after dinner with the newspaper that he hadn't had time to read during the day. He had his favorite TV programs, and looked forward to watching them.

The two of them might go to a movie on the rare occasion during the week, but Bruce really preferred to stay at home. They seldom quarreled, and he usually gave in to Leslie when she wanted to do something that didn't interest him. He was not handsome in a Hollywood style, but was attractive enough. The couple had had two daughters who were now adults, and married with their own families.

Leslie's grown children lived miles away, so she only saw them two or three times a year. Her small circle of friends began to dwindle, as well. The days became longer and the nights even lonelier. That's what made her decide to make an appointment to visit the Palm Beach Palace. She wanted to see what the place was like, and what it could offer to lift her spirits.

The moment she walked through the wide entrance, Leslie was struck by how beautiful it was! She entered a huge foyer with neatly placed overstuffed chairs and loveseats. There was an ornate rug on the floor, and tapestries hanging on the walls. At one side, sat a cozy bar where she imagined pleasant evenings meeting and chatting with new friends. Bouquets of flowers decorated each area. There was a library, a computer room, an exercise room, a card room, a cinema for evening films, and a large auditorium with a stage for performances.

After she saw the common areas, she toured the residents' apartments, which seemed to be quite comfortable. There were one-bedroom and two-bedroom units; each included a living room and kitchen. Through a sliding glass door was a balcony overlooking the pool below. Palm trees encircled the pool, some even around the balcony. She was delighted. Her resident guide told her she could rent for a year on a trial basis. But, for Leslie, there was really no point in thinking about it anymore — this would be a place for her to meet other people, and give her a chance to do things that she had not had time to do during her married life. She decided that it was not necessary to mull it over; this was the right thing to do. And the more time she gave herself to think about it, the harder it would be to make a decision. So she said, "Yes I'll take it," went home, put the house up for sale and started to pack.

Her house was in excellent condition so it sold in three short weeks. Of course, she gave a lot of stuff away, but she kept the better items to furnish the new apartment. Eventually all the details of relocating were sorted out, and in no time at all, Leslie moved in to the Palm Beach Palace.

After the decision to move, Leslie felt a great sense of relief. She didn't have to shop for food any more. She would have her meals in the huge dining room, and a reliable maid would come weekly to keep her small, but comfortable apartment clean and tidy.

The day she moved in, she felt a weight lift off her shoulders—no more big house to clean and manage, and no more cooking. She could do whatever she wanted. If she felt like socializing, she could go downstairs and meet people. If she wanted to be alone, she could stay in her apartment or sit on her balcony. Now, at last, she was responsible for herself and herself alone.

When she started to unpack her luggage, she was thrilled to find an enormous walk-in closet with racks large enough for all her clothes, plus built-in shelves for her shoes and purses. Leslie unpacked for about an hour, then looked at her watch—it was time for dinner.

She walked down to the dining room. It was huge and had tables that seated two, four and six people. She was assigned to a table for six. Five seats were already occupied—three men and two women. The sixth place was waiting for her.

Before Leslie sat down, she said to the group, "Hello, I'm Leslie Harper and I'm delighted to be assigned to this table." The five people looked at her. As she sat down, one of the men stood up and extended his hand to her, "Welcome Leslie," he said. "My name is Albert, but they call me Big Al." Indeed, he was big—he stood at least 6 foot, 3 inches tall and must have weighed well over 200 pounds. He had lost a good deal of his hair, and what was left was mostly gray. He gave Leslie a big smile, and she could tell right away that he would be a good friend in the future.

Then a second man stood up. "Hi, Leslie, glad to meet you. My name is Charles, but you can call me Charlie anytime you want." Charlie stood close to 6 feet tall, and was much slimmer than Big Al. His hair was thinning, and some silver was forming at the temples. He was not exactly handsome, but very pleasant to look at. In addition to that, he appeared to have a nice disposition. She liked him at once.

The third man didn't bother to get up or shake her hand. "I'm Frank. I hope you enjoy your stay at the Palace," he said. And without the smile the other two men had given her—he simply nodded. Leslie noticed he had a scooter at his side. She felt that the other two men might become her friends, but she didn't think that Frank would ever want to be friends with her, nor she with him.

Leslie glanced at the two women. One of them gave her a big smile, and said, "Hi Leslie, I'm Susan." She had shoulder-length blonde hair and blue eyes. She was attractive, and Leslie felt that she could easily form a pleasant friendship with her.

The other woman barely looked up, but said somewhat tersely, "Hi, I'm Betty. Glad you're here." Betty had short dark brown hair, and looked to be in her 70s. She wore a hint of a frown, and knitted her eyebrows as she dug into her purse. She didn't seem to be interested in anyone or anything other than what was in her purse, which was open on her lap. Her hands fumbled busily as she looked for something that she seemed unable to find. Leslie noticed that both women were clothed in lovely looking tops, but since they were sitting she couldn't tell if they were wearing pants or skirts.

Leslie sat down in her chair and looked at the group of people she would be dining with during her stay at the Palace. It was a nice group, she thought. She then noticed Frank reach down beside him into his scooter, and pull out a bottle of wine. "Here, give me your glass, Leslie," he said. She noticed all the others at the table had glasses of wine at their place setting. "Here's to you, Leslie. I hope you enjoy your stay at the Palace." Frank raised his glass and said, "Santé." The others raised their glasses, as did Leslie, and they all chimed in, "Santé." After they toasted, Susan whispered to Leslie, "Frank brings a bottle of wine to our table every night."

This was a wonderful way to start a new life for myself, Leslie thought—a chance to have new friends. She knew she had made the right choice to move into the Palm Beach Palace.

CHAPTER TWO

Table for Six

They all picked up their menus—which had a vast number of selections from which to choose. There were several courses, which made a decision difficult. There was soup or salad or both, if desired, plus, a choice of several different meat or fish courses. And, of course, there was dessert to end the meal.

Betty sat silently as Leslie and Susan started to talk. Leslie knew that she and Susan would most certainly become friends. The men at the table carried on their own conversations.

Then Charlie leaned over toward Leslie and asked, "Where are you from?"

"Well, I was born in Boston, and then moved to New York," answered Leslie. "After I finished college, I landed a job in an art gallery. That is where I met my husband, Bruce. We fell in love, and within a year we were married."

Meanwhile, Leslie watched as Betty produced a paper towel from her purse, and proceeded to wipe every piece of the flatware in front of her. Leslie asked, "Why are you cleaning off your flatware?"

"Well, you can never be completely sure that they're clean," Betty answered in a suspicious tone. "I saw a waiter pick up a fork that had fallen on the floor, and he put it right back on the table. For that reason, I make it a habit to wipe my fork, knife, and spoon just to make sure that they're clean." And she proceeded to do just that. Just then, the waiter stepped up to take their order. He had overheard Betty's derogatory comment.

"Excuse me, ma'am, but what you've just described is something we would never do here at the Palace. We hold the highest standards of cleanliness. The waiter who did that must have been an outsider hired for the one day. Now, if we may proceed with your dinner, are you all ready to place your order?" They all nodded, and smiled, except for Betty who scowled slightly, and obviously didn't buy the waiter's explanation.

After they ordered, Leslie looked at Susan, who gave a little grin. "Betty wipes her utensils every night," Susan said. "It keeps her busy. But, Leslie, tell us a little more about yourself. How come you chose to live at the Palace?" asked Susan.

Leslie laughed. "I'm probably here for the same reasons the rest of you are. I want to enjoy life while I'm still healthy enough to get around. I don't want to be burdened by household duties, and I want to have my days filled with activities and friendships."

Al interjected, "You're so right, Leslie—that's why I'm here. When my wife died, I found it very difficult to live alone in a big house. I've been at the Palace for almost a year, and I know that I'm better off than I would be living on my own. There's a lot to do here if you want to do it. I was even in a play they produced here. Even though I'm not an actor, it was a wonderful experience for me."

Everyone around the table became happily engaged in small talk, except for Betty, who was still intently foraging through the contents of her purse. Leslie looked at her and wondered. What in the world was in her purse that was so interesting? After all, she had already wiped off her knife, fork and spoon due to doubts about the sanitary habits of the help. Leslie couldn't figure it out. Regardless, she attempted to strike up a dialog with Betty to get her mind off her purse.

"Where are you from, Betty?" Leslie asked her.

"I'm from Canada," Betty answered.

"From Canada?"

"Yeah, it gets real cold there in the wintertime. So I'm what they call a snowbird," Betty responded.

"So, when do you usually come down?"

"Oh, we typically arrive the beginning of November."

"And how long do you stay?"

"I'm here until April."

"And then you go back? You keep a place here at the Palace and you keep a place in Canada?"

"That's right," Betty said.

"That must be expensive."

"Well, it is, in a way. But it gets me out of the hot, hot weather in Florida and the cold, cold weather in Canada."

"That makes sense," Leslie replied. Then she asked, "Are you married, Betty?"

"My husband died six years ago."

"I'm sorry to hear that," consoled Leslie. "Do you have any children?"

Betty replied, "Yes, I have two daughters and a son who is a doctor."

"Where does your son live?"

"He lives in Canada."

"So, I guess you only see him when you go back?" asked Leslie?

"Oh, he tries to come down once in a while. But he's married and has children, and his practice keeps him quite occupied."

"And your daughters? Do you see them often?"

"Yes, I do," said Betty. "They both live in New York and they come down to Florida quite often. But I've made friends here. So life is good."

"Of course, there are the people here. But I don't mind being by myself. I like to read, I like to walk, and I love to look at the ocean. So I'm okay. I don't know what I'll do when I get really old—I suppose I'll need care then, but for now I'm fine." And then she returned to fumbling in her purse.

The waiter brought their dinner, and as the group began to eat, Big Al asked Leslie, "Do you know anybody in the Palace?" Leslie shook her head. "No, I don't know a soul. You're the only people I've met. I'm sure I'll meet more friendly folks like you all, but in the mean time I'll find things to do. Maybe I'll learn a new language. Maybe I'll study Spanish and then go to Spain. I've always wanted to visit Spain."

Big Al laughed. "Yes, I can just see you there doing the tango."

Everyone laughed and Leslie said, "Why not? I love to dance. Do they have dancing here at the Palace?"

"No real dances. But we do have a show every Saturday night."

Leslie perked up, "Really, a show every week?"

"Yes, they bring in a singer or a comedian who sings or tells jokes. Sometimes it's hard to find a seat because the event is so popular."

"Oh, I would get there early. I love shows."

Charlie added, "Don't expect too much, Leslie. Like Betty said, it's just some guy singing or telling corny jokes. They often repeat the same performers year after year. I should know because I've been here for over five years. When you get older, you don't expect to go out much."

After a brief silence, Frank raised a glass and said, "Let's drink to the shows here at the Palace. May they grow bigger and better as we grow older and better!"

They all raised their glasses and chanted, "Santé!"

As the evening progressed, Leslie felt more and more comfortable. She couldn't believe she'd only been there one day. She thought it was extremely interesting to hear the stories that some of the people told. All these people who didn't know each other before they came to the Palace were now good friends. Some were more outgoing than others, but there was always someone you could sit and talk to if you wanted.

When dinner was over, the men rose to leave the table and Susan came over to Leslie. "Would you like to go to the cinema tonight, Leslie? They are showing a good film."

Leslie smiled at Susan, and said, "Thanks so much, but I haven't unpacked my things yet and there is a great big closet waiting to be filled. I'd be delighted to go another night. It's been so lovely meeting you all. Good night."

Indeed, there was a large walk-in closet that Leslie was eager to fill. But she thought to herself, "Tonight, I'm just going to relax and think about the days ahead at the Palace." So she went up to her apartment, intending to unpack just the essentials. But when she entered her apartment, the attractive balcony beckoned to her, and she couldn't resist the urge to see it. She sat down on a cushioned patio chair and looked out into the night sky. The moon was shining brightly. Palm trees encircled the pool area, and a palm tree grew so close to her balcony that she could almost touch its branches. The gleaming pool lights on the patio, the glowing moon and gently waving palm trees entranced Leslie. This was her version of a perfect Florida evening. "I'll unpack tomorrow," she thought. "I just can't leave this wonderful sight.

What a nice evening it's been," she mused. "I'm so glad I sold the house. I know Bruce would never have wanted me to do it, but I have my life to live now. I'll try as hard as I can to do it my way. I don't know how many years I have ahead of me, but I want them filled with happiness."

She sighed with contentment, and almost purred like a cat. She was happy. Reluctantly, she left the balcony and started to prepare for bed. She was tired, but she was happier now than she had been since Bruce's death. She was beginning a new life and she wondered what her future would be like at the Palm Beach Palace.

CHAPTER THREE

Breakfast Friends

The next morning when Leslie woke up, she stretched
her arms and looked around her apartment. Her
bedroom was large, and had a bathroom next to it
where there was a shower and all the facilities she
would need. There was one TV set in the bedroom,
and another one in the living room, so she could
watch television in either room. The living room
was a good size for a small apartment. It had a
loveseat and two comfortable chairs. Area lighting
included accent lamps, as well as a ceiling light. The
balcony was off of the living room. As she stepped
out to look down at the pool area, she saw some of
the Palace residents already lounging around the
pool. There was a small kitchen next to the living
room with a refrigerator, stove, and microwave.
Dishes were stored in the cupboards and flatware
in the drawers. There were several pots and pans if

she wanted to cook. A small powder room was off the hallway leading to the apartment door.

Yes, it was true—it wasn't a dream, she thought to herself. She had really moved into the Palm Beach Palace.

She decided to go down for breakfast. She showered, pulled on jeans and a T-shirt, and selected a pair of sandals. Then she went down to the dining room.

Leslie assumed she would be sitting at the same table that had been assigned to her the previous evening. But when she went into the dining room, she saw Susan sitting at a table for four with two other women. There was an empty chair at their table, and Leslie went over to say good morning to Susan. She pointed to the empty chair and asked, "May I join you?"

Susan replied, "But of course. I want you to meet my two friends here—Mildred and Pearl."

Leslie sat down and said, "Hello Pearl. Hello Mildred—glad to meet you." They both smiled at her and said, "It's a pleasure to meet you too, Leslie."

The three women seemed to have already ordered their breakfast, so Leslie summoned the waiter with a nod. He came over, and she ordered orange juice, cereal, French toast and coffee.

Then she turned to Pearl and asked, "Where are you from?" Pearl answered, "New York. A lot of the people here are from New York. They come for the warmer climate."

"And you, Mildred?" asked Leslie, "Where are you from?"

Mildred replied, "Believe it or not, I was born in Florida, and I've lived here all my life. Where are you from, Leslie?"

Leslie replied, "I'm from Boston. After I married Bruce, my late husband, his career led us to many other places. We raised our children in Boston. He had his MBA, and we travelled quite a bit because of his work with a large firm. After he retired, we decided to move to Florida. We made new friends, but then he had a stroke and became so ill that nothing could save him.

"I tried living alone in the house, but it was too much for me. There were too many memories of Bruce, and too much housekeeping to keep up. I needed companionship—I needed friends. I used to walk past the Palm Beach Palace frequently, and often wondered what it was like inside. One day, I decided to see, and made an appointment to discover what the Palace was like on the inside, as well as the outside. I liked what I saw; put my house up for sale, and then I rented an apartment here. And I'm glad I did."

The dining room was almost deserted at this point—it looked to Leslie like people ate early in order to give themselves a nice long day. She looked around the dining room and liked what she saw. It was certainly different from what she had seen the night before when it had been crowded with people. Now it was nearly empty—a big, pleasant room with many windows. So far, Leslie thought, "I like how I feel about this place. I really think I'm going to enjoy my life here."

As they were eating, Susan said to Leslie, "On Saturdays we always have entertainment in the evenings. I hope you will come sometime. It's usually not a 5-star show, but it's something to do, and sometimes the entertainer is really good. But most times, it's just the usual songs and a couple of corny jokes. Perhaps we can go some Saturday."

Leslie said, "Yes, I would love to. Let's do it in a few weeks. We can meet at the entrance of the auditorium before the show starts, okay?"

Susan replied, "Of course, the show usually starts at 8 pm, but the seats are filled up much earlier."

After breakfast, Leslie went to the front desk. The Palm Beach Palace was run almost like a hotel. There was someone at the front desk nearly 24 hours a day.

There was also a security man on duty that made sure that everything was in order. Leslie asked for the Palace's activity brochure. It listed all the events for the month. Leslie decided to sit at the pool to read it.

She selected a white wicker chair, and was delighted to find out that it was a rocker. She loved rockers. She checked off some the activities listed for the week, and found several that she was interested in. There were exercise classes, art classes; there was a drama group and a walking group. She noted that there was a schedule for bus outings. One day the bus would take residents who had signed up to a mall for shopping; another day, the bus would take people to a pharmacy or a supermarket. And on other days, it would be available to transport residents to medical and dental appointments. Leslie thought, *How wonderful! I don't need a car. I don't need to buy food. I don't need to clean my own apartment. It's all taken care of. Yes indeed, I did the right thing by moving here.*

She noticed that there was a drama group meeting every Wednesday, and decided that she'd like to attend the next audition. Leslie had acted in a number of plays, and she thought it would be fun to be a part of the next production at the Palace. This could be fun, she thought.

CHAPTER FOUR

A Buzz in the Palace

The next day while she sat by the pool, Leslie noticed a man nearby in a lounge chair reading a book. He looked up and saw her looking at him, and then came over to sit in a chair near her. He said, "Are you new to the Palace?"

Leslie replied, "Yes, I am. I'm Leslie Harper."

"I'm Norman. Norman O'Reilly."

"Well hello," said Leslie "How long have you lived here?"

"Oh, about two years," he responded. "I came here when my wife died. I'm not one for housekeeping—I like having things done for me." Norman looked to be about seventy, she thought. He was clean-shaven, his hair neatly brushed. He was wearing a black T-shirt and white shorts. He had long legs, and wore sandals.

"So," said Norman, "What brought you here?"

Leslie said, "Probably the same thing that brought you here. My husband died, and I didn't want to live alone in a big house. I think this is a wonderful opportunity for people like us to live as best we can in our declining years."

Norman said, "Please don't say 'declining.' I think these past years are some of the best I've ever had. I don't have anyone to tell me what to do. I'm lucky enough to have money to stay here. I'm not rich, but I did put aside enough money for myself before retiring. My children are capable of taking care of themselves now. So I don't worry about them, and they don't worry about me."

"Good for you," said Leslie.

Then, Norman said, "I don't know whether you have heard, but we have a new director here, and I think he's going to make some changes to some of the things we've gotten used to."

Leslie responded in surprise. "What do you mean changes? What are they going to do?"

"Well," said Norman, "I don't know exactly what they have planned, but I heard through the grapevine that we're not going to have waiters for our breakfast."

"What does that mean?" asked Leslie. "You mean we're not going to have our breakfast served to us anymore?"

"Well, I'm not sure, but it seems that way."

"Well, how will we get breakfast?"

"Self-serve," he said. "I think they will have things on the tables and you will have to go get them for yourself."

"Oh no," said Leslie, "I like to sit at my table and receive what I've ordered."

"Well, maybe it's just a rumor and won't really happen, I don't know. But I've heard a number of people talking about it. I'm just passing this along to you."

Leslie stood up. "It was nice meeting you, Norman. I hope you're wrong about the rules being changed. But, no matter what happens, I think we'll be able to cope with whatever happens. I've got to go and finish settling into my apartment. I've just recently arrived, so I have a lot to do still."

"Nice meeting you, too," said Norman. "Maybe we can have dinner some night."

"Maybe we can," replied Leslie. And she went off to start getting her things put away.

On her way up to her apartment, she saw a small woman with a tiara on her head. Leslie smiled at the woman, and she smiled back. Leslie wondered who she was and why she was wearing a tiara as well as so much jewelry. She decided to ask Susan and her friends if they knew anything about her.

So, that night at dinner, she told her tablemates about the encounter with the tiara-clad woman. They all laughed. Frank said, "Oh, we call her The Princess."

Leslie asked, "The Princess?"

Again, they all laughed. Then Frank explained, "She thought she was supposed to marry the Prince of Wales. She said he had proposed to her. But then that horrible woman Wallace Simpson came along, and took him away from her." Again, they all laughed.

Frank said, "That calls for some more wine." He pulled out his bottle and poured wine into their glasses. They all raised their glasses and said, "Santé! Here's to The Princess."

Back in her apartment, the following day, Leslie had begun to hang pictures and decorate her place. She loved so much about her new space, especially her big closet. She had never had a walk-in closet and this was special joy to her. There were shelves and lots of racks where she could hang her pantsuits. She could put her sweaters and tops on shelves and hang up her dresses. There were also shelves for her shoes and purses.

After tidying-up her apartment, she went down to lunch. There was no scheduled time for lunch and it was served in a smaller dining room. Lunch consisted of sandwiches or salads. For the time being, the waiters still served the food to individual guests. She was thankful that she didn't have to serve herself—yet, she thought if what Norman told her was really true.

After that she made a visit the library. She checked over the books. Nothing exciting, she thought—I've got my own books. But there were magazines, as well as one copy of the Palm Beach Post, which someone was reading. How could it be possible that there was just one newspaper? Leslie asked herself? She would inquire at the desk why there was only the one copy.

She walked by a computer room and she decided to go in and use a computer for a while. But, before she knew it, it was time to dress for dinner. She went back to her apartment, changed her clothes and then went down to her assigned place at the table for six where she sat with Susan, Betty, Frank, Al, and Charlie.

Again, the wine bottle was produced and poured into everyone's glass. They all raised their glasses and said, "Santé!" And then the waiter came to take their dinner order.

"How was your day?" Charlie asked Leslie.

"Oh, it was great," she responded. "I explored the building and unpacked everything. I think I love this place, and I love this table. I'm glad I came."

The menu listed so many good things—Leslie ordered the soup-of-the-day, a small salad, and roast beef with a baked potato and broccoli. Everybody ordered dessert, so she did too, apple pie with ice cream and coffee. The food was delicious.

When the meal was over, Susan said, "Time to go, Leslie. Let's go see the show."

Oh! I completely forgot we'd decided to go tonight. Let me run upstairs and quickly change. I'll meet you at the entrance!"

A few minutes later, Leslie and Susan walked into the auditorium together, which was almost completely filled. There were many walkers lining the outside aisles. After all, the Palm Beach Palace was erected for seniors, and sooner or later, people found that walking was a little difficult without something to hold onto. So many of the residents had walkers, and a few sat in wheelchairs. Then there were also people like Susan and Leslie who could get about quite easily without any assistance. They found two seats near the back of the auditorium and the show began.

The lights dimmed, the stage was lighted, and a man came out and said, "Good evening folks. I'm so glad to be here. I was here last year—remember me? I'm the one with a head full of hair, and none on my face." He was wearing a dark blue suit with a large red kerchief in his breast pocket. He didn't look like an entertainer—he looked like he could have been a used car salesman, as indeed he had been. He loved entertaining people. His voice wasn't too bad, and he had half a dozen jokes that he told over and over again. He loved to sing, and he encouraged the audience to sing along with him. Sometimes he would stop singing and ask, "How many here are from New Jersey?" And a lot of arms would go up in the air. "How many are here from Massachusetts? Hey—that's where I'm from? None of you? Well, that's too bad, it's a great state." He was having fun doing his performance. He had always wanted to be an entertainer, and now he was one.

"I'm thrilled to be back here again. So, let's hear it for the Palace, folks!" Everyone applauded.

His fee was not high—he probably would have done this for free. But he had a pension, and this small amount that the Palace paid him would pay for travel expenses including car upkeep and gas with a little left over to help with household bills.

He turned on his stereo and the sound of an orchestra came on. He started to sing, and some people in the audience sang along with him. In between the songs, he told a few jokes. Some of the audience groaned at one of the jokes—it was an old corny one he told every time he appeared at the Palace. The show lasted about two hours, and he was applauded loudly when it ended.

Leslie said to Susan, "That really wasn't much of a show, was it?"

Susan responded, "I told you not to expect too much. That's what we have here, but it's something to do. The crowd likes it. Well, I think I'm going to turn in."

Leslie said, "I am too." They got in the elevator and Susan got off at her floor. Leslie got off at her own floor and walked to her apartment.

It's been quite a day, Leslie thought, I feel like I've been here a whole month. I'm already used to this place. I think I'm going to enjoy living here.

She unlocked her apartment door, went in and locked it behind her, and then prepared for bed. Again, she went out on her balcony while she was in her pajamas. The moon shone brightly. The palm trees fluttered. She went back inside and got into bed. She stretched her legs and arms and was happy to be in her new quarters.

CHAPTER FIVE

Drama Club

The next morning, Leslie showered, dressed, and went down for breakfast. She had decided that after breakfast she would explore the Palace a little more to see what else it offered, and what interested her the most.

When she entered the dining room, she saw Norman sitting by himself at a table having his breakfast. She didn't see Susan any place, so she went over to Norman and said, "Do you mind if I join you?"

"Please do. Please sit down," replied Norman. "There's been more talk about the dining staff situation. I heard that they're planning to dismiss all but one waiter."

"Oh, no! How on earth can one waiter take care of a whole dining room full of guests?" asked Leslie.

"Well that's the point—they won't need waiters because everything will be self-serve."

Leslie stared at him a bit astonished. "I still don't think it's fair. It's a little like false advertizing." she said. "One of the reasons I came here was because I was assured of three good meals a day. Good food and good service."

"Well," said Norman, "that may be a thing of the past. This new director has sent out word that a lot of the foods will be eliminated, also. For example, while we can now order omelets, cereals, pancakes and waffles for our breakfast, that may all be changed."

"Oh, so now the menu will be shortened as well? What will our choices be, say, for breakfast?" Leslie asked.

"There will probably be a table where you go to get your cereal and juices. And there will be a chef who will be able to make eggs for you in any form you want," Norman said.

"I don't like that," replied Leslie.

"I don't either," responded Norman. "I've been thinking about what we can do."

"What can we do? As residents, I think we have a say in the matter." Leslie persisted.

"We can go on strike."

"What do you mean?"

"I mean we can insist that we keep the waiters we have now, and that we also are served the same food we have now," explained Norman.

"How would you arrange that?"

"I have a plan," he replied. "If we all get together, we can outwit this new director."

"And how would we do that?" asked Leslie.

"I think that if all the residents at the Palace come down, and sit at their table to express their concerns, this new director will have to change his mind, and let us have what we want for breakfast. I know it's a small thing, but we are paying good money to be here, and we expect to eat well," Norman said.

"So how will you let everyone know about the plan?" asked Leslie?

"I will send word to all the residents to be here tomorrow morning at nine o'clock, and sit at their tables. They will just sit here without ordering anything while all our waiters are still here."

"And you think that will make a difference to the director?" asked Leslie.

"Oh yes—I do. I think it will make a big difference. I'm going to leave notes under everyone's door. I've appointed people from every floor to put notes under the residents' doors and so we'll all meet tomorrow at nine."

Leslie looked at him bewildered. "You think just sitting here will make the difference?" she asked.

"Yes, I do. I do indeed." Norman assured her.

"Well, I certainly hope your plan works," Leslie conceded.

Then Norman, seeing the topic was upsetting Leslie, said, "What are your plans for this beautiful sunny day?"

"Norman, believe it or not, I still have not finished settling into my apartment. I've been so busy enjoying my new friends and the activities here at the Palace that I have yet to unpack all my boxes. So, I plan to do that today!"

"Okay," chuckled Norman. "You have a good time unpacking, while I digest my breakfast out at the shady pool."

"Thanks a lot," joked Leslie back.

Reluctantly, Leslie returned to her apartment to continue unpacking. She started putting her clothes into the spacious closet. Leslie had never had such a big closet. There was a place for everything; shelves for sweaters, shelves for purses, shelves for shoes as well as for her pants. It was such a pleasure to have ample space and detailed organization in her closet.

There were hangers for dresses and even hooks for scarves and jewelry.

She soon tired of that and decided to rest on the balcony to enjoy the warmth of the sunshine and the quiet. All was serene. Before she knew it, it was time for lunch. She also remembered today was the day she would audition for the community play.

After lunch, she went to the drama room and found about twelve people there, with more women than men.

The director of the group was a gal who had been in the theatrical business, and was now living at the Palace. She had a number of scripts with her, and doled them out to the people present.

They sat around a table and each one reviewed their script silently. Leslie found a part she felt she could do well, and asked if she could audition for it. The director said, "First, let's all read the script aloud. Leslie—why don't we start with you?"

So the group started reading the various parts of the play one after the other. Some read well, some stumbled over words, and bit by bit the drama director could see who was suited for each of the seven parts.

Leslie got the role she had read and liked, and the six other parts were given to other people. Those who were without parts left and the people who had been selected now sat around the table and started to read the play.

It was fun, Leslie thought. She had always been interested in the theatre. She enjoyed reading the play. The drama director told them when they would meet again, and advised them to take their scripts back to their apartments to study their lines.

The play was scheduled to be presented in six weeks, and it was no small job for them to memorize their parts. Rehearsals started, and Leslie attended every one of them. Leslie loved going to the rehearsals, and looked forward to the final performance.

From time to time Leslie suggested some changes to the production, such as using the lights in between acts because there was no curtain on the stage. The director was delighted to have someone like Leslie to improve the details.

Everything seemed to go smoothly until at the next to the last rehearsal, when one of the women in the cast stood up, and started to leave the room.

The director asked, "Where are you going?"

The woman responded, "I am a professional—I don't need to rehearse this much."

"Well, professionals don't act like this. You don't need to be in the play. You may leave your script and excuse yourself." she said.

It was so late in the rehearsal process that the director had to decide who would take the vacant space left by the disgruntled actress. The director knew that she needed to proceed with the rehearsals. So, she turned to Leslie and asked, "Leslie, can you take this part in addition to your own? I'd love for you to step in for this open part." Leslie agreed and was thrilled to be of help.

The following week was opening night. Everyone was prepared and had perfected their parts. The night of the performance went splendidly. The auditorium was filled to capacity. Even though there were a few slip-ups, the performers enjoyed acting and the audience enjoyed watching the play. Each cast member was given a yellow rose, and the director was given a bouquet of flowers. Leslie felt so at home with the other actors.

The days were speeding by so quickly, Leslie couldn't believe that she had been at the Palm Beach Palace for only three months. She felt as if she had been at the Palace for years instead of weeks. Whatever would she have done if she had remained in her house? This was the smartest thing she could have done at her stage in life.

At the same time, she was getting to meet more of Susan's friends and sat frequently at a table beside the pool. She and her friends would talk about many things: mostly about their lives, husbands and children. Some of them had never worked, or held careers outside of the home. Some of them had. They all felt so close to each other and formed a tight group. Some had had good lives with their husbands, others, not so good. Some had one child each, some had two or three. Some were on good terms with their children, some not so good. As they talked they grew closer together. Some talked about how they had started out with financial problems. Some of the women had husbands who had done very well, and that's why they were able to stay at the Palace. Others had children who were helping them out. All together at this time in their lives they were living comfortably. Their health for the most part was good, and they had no real problems in maintaining their way of life. Most of them were in their early seventies; a few were in their eighties. They all agreed with the quote that someone once said, "Never mind tomorrow. Yesterday is history and tomorrow is a mystery. So, let's just live for today in the present."

CHAPTER SIX

Mall Excursion

One time at dinner while they waited for their food, Leslie looked around and noticed that everyone was well-dressed for the evening. Shorts (for men or women) were not allowed in the dining room during the evening meal. She glanced around at the occupied tables and noticed how nice some of the women looked. They wore lovely dresses or tops and pants with coordinating jewelry.

Since Bruce had died, Leslie hadn't thought about her wardrobe because she did not go out very often. She realized that one of these days she would have to take the bus that was scheduled to go to a mall so she could shop for some new clothes. She wanted to look as attractive as she could—as good as the other women looked.

Leslie decided she would have to update her wardrobe and that a trip to the mall was in order. So she put her name down to reserve a space since the bus could only take 30 people. She chose a beautiful day to take the residents' bus to one of the local malls. She was sure she would find just the outfits to make her look as well put together as the others did at dinner. She was also curious to see what the mall looked like. The bus was slated to visit two different malls that day with a stop first at one mall and then the other. Passengers were told where and when the bus would pick them up to take them back to the Palace.

Leslie strolled along inside the mall where there was a large department store and many smaller retail shops. After trying on a few things, she did end up getting three new outfits. "That should do it," Leslie thought. One of the ensembles struck her fancy so much, that she had the clerk take the tags off and she put it on to wear for the rest of the day. Then she looked at her watch, and found that it was time for the bus to pick her up. So she went outside to stand at the designated departure spot.

Leslie waited and waited, but the bus didn't come. She couldn't see any of the other Palace passengers who had gotten off the bus with her. She thought perhaps she should go to the other mall, which was walking distance away. Sure enough, the bus was there waiting for her. She had mistaken where she was supposed to catch the bus to return to the Palace. They all teased her and joked about it. They decided to buy her a compass for her next outing. And they also complimented her on how nice she looked!

After dinner, on her way to the elevator, Leslie again saw the lady wearing the tiara walking down the corridor. The woman wore not just any tiara, but a golden encrusted mini crown, as well as multiple strings of beads around her neck. This was truly the oddest thing that Leslie had laid her eyes on. She started to greet the woman out of curiosity, but the 'princess' hurried on as if she didn't want an intrusion.

Intrigued and undeterred, Leslie decided to ask the princess a little bit about her life. So as they crossed paths in the hall, Leslie asked, "Do you have a minute? I'd love to talk to you." The 'princess' answered, "What do you want to talk about?"

"I wonder about your life. You seem so different from the other residents here."

"Well, I am different. I've had a very disappointing life. I was born into a royal family, but they never acknowledged me. They treated me the same as my other sisters, but I knew I was different. So, I left home when I was 17 and I married into a royal family. Then I met Prince Charles. He was my type. I fell in love with him immediately."

"Let's sit down," Said Leslie. "This is very interesting."

So they went to the computer room because it was very quiet.

"Tell me more about you," Leslie asked.

"Well," said the princess, "There are some things I can tell, there are some things I can't. They are sacred to me."

"Then, just tell me what you want to tell me. I won't pry." Leslie said.

"Ok, what do you want to know?"

"Tell me about yourself growing up as a young girl." Leslie said.

"Well," said the princess. "I had three sisters and one brother. They treated me just like Cinderella was treated by her step-sisters. I knew who I was. I knew I was different because I had been adopted. I was descended from royalty. There was a family related to the tsar of Russia. And you know they were all killed except for one: the great Duchess Olga. I was her child. We were in an automobile accident and I was the only survivor. So this family adopted me. They had two girls who treated me like Cinderella. They ordered me around: 'Do this. Do that. Go here. Go there.' When I told them I was royalty, they laughed at me.

"Then one day, I was in London and I saw Prince Charles. Oh, he was so handsome. I fell in love at once. He looked at me and gave me a big smile. But he was married to Diana then, and he wouldn't do anything to hurt his marriage. So I waited until Diana was killed. I know he is going to call me one of these days. That's why I wear a tiara.

"My siblings grew up and were married, but I was waiting for Charles. I knew he didn't love Diana, but me instead. But he had to marry someone who could produce an heir for him. And then Diana died in that auto accident and I was certain he would come for me. I'm still waiting because I know he loves me. And that's why I'm at the palace. Any day he may come for me. I even keep a bag packed. I am royalty and wear the crown."

Leslie listened with amazement. *Did the princess really believe this? Was she really waiting for Prince Charles? Did she really think he would come?* Leslie stared at the princess. *Did she just have an overactive imagination or really believe it? Probably both. She believed it and had an imagination beyond belief.*

"I'm afraid that's all the time I have for you dear. So I bid you a good day and hope to see you again," said the 'princess.'

Leslie sat in the computer room for a few minutes trying to collect her thoughts. This was such an unusual place. She felt that she was now residing in a very peculiar place. There was the man who brought wine to dinner every night. They toasted "Santé" several times during meals. There's the drama going on about our waiter staff. And now this strange woman who thinks she'd destined to marry Prince Charles.

But the unpredictability is what she liked about the place. What fun she was having. Every new day was different. Just imagine if she had stayed all alone in her old house. She would not be enjoying the lovely and interesting new life she had made for herself.

CHAPTER SEVEN

Poolside Conversation

One day, Leslie walked out to the pool area and saw Susan sitting with Pearl and Mildred. They looked very relaxed. So she decided to order a sandwich and salad, and then sit by the pool for a while.

She walked over to where they were sitting and asked, "May I join you?"

"By all means," Susan said. "Draw up a chair."

"Isn't this weather great?" asked Leslie.

"That's Florida for you," replied Pearl. "That's why we all came down here. It's the weather that drew us here."

"Do you have any children?" Leslie asked.

"Yes, I have two. One is in New York and the other is in New Jersey," said Pearl.

"How about you?" Leslie turned to Mildred.

"I have one," she replied. "I don't get to see him often, but he's a great son. He calls me once a week.

I wish I could see him more often, but he has a wife and children of his own. Between his work and his family, he cannot get away too often. And how about you, Leslie? Do you have any children?"

"Yes, I have two girls. They live near each other and call me all the time. They both work, so they cannot get away very often. When they can, they come here to see me," Leslie responded.

"How long were you married, Leslie?" Mildred asked.

"I was married to Bruce for 42 years. He was a good man, but that didn't lead to a very exciting life. He didn't like to talk very much. He was content to stay at home after work. And after he had his dinner, he liked to watch the news on TV along with anything else that might interest him. He liked to take walks occasionally, but other than that, he didn't like to go out much."

"Did you work at all while you were married?" asked Mildred.

"Yes, I worked in an art gallery. Not full-time, of course, but I love art. It helped me get through the week, and it helped me meet some interesting people who used to come into the gallery."

There was a brief pause, and then Susan said, "It is difficult running a household, raising children, and being a dutiful wife."

Mildred responded, "What do you mean 'a dutiful wife?' A wife is a wife—she has a life of her own. If she keeps the house tidy and prepares decent dinners, she should have a little time on her own."

Leslie laughed, "That's the trouble. A lot of women don't know what to do with themselves. They play bridge, they go shopping. But many don't enhance their lives with anything really meaningful."

"Well," said Susan, "When you get married, when you say 'I do,' that means 'I will' try to make my marriage as pleasant as possible. Some men encourage their wives to make lives of their own. But in our days, most men hadn't a clue as to what to do in the kitchen."

Pearl laughed. "That's true. My husband tried to make some soup once. He took out a pressure cooker, put in the ingredients and turned on the pot. In a little while, the pressure cooker burst open and everything exploded onto the ceiling." They all laughed. "So, I think I'm better off when he doesn't come into the kitchen."

"You know," Pearl said, "if you're lucky, marriage can be a good thing. You have a companion for life, if he's that kind of man. Mine wasn't. He was happy to make a good wage—he always had a good job. He loved his house, he loved his children, I hope he loved me—but there wasn't that closeness that I had hoped for before we were married."

Susan sighed. "Yeah—I know what you mean. Before I was married, my mother said that all a man wanted was to have sex. She told me that you'll have to do what they want. She said men want sex, but women don't."

Leslie laughed, "That's crazy. I loved having sex with Bruce. He was a great lover."

Susan looked at her. "Boy, were you lucky. My mother couldn't wait to get twin beds. It took a long time to convince my father that that's what they should do. I don't know what he did after that. I know if you're lucky, it's a beautiful part of marriage."

"Amen," said Leslie, "It's a beautiful part of marriage, if you're lucky."

"How did you two meet, Leslie?" Susan asked.

Leslie laughed. "It was a tennis racket that brought us together." The other three women looked at each other and laughed, too.

Mildred asked, "A tennis racket? What do you mean by that?"

"Well," Leslie said, "my family belonged to a club that had a tennis court, and I used to play tennis there occasionally. I went there one morning, had a game and decided to go home. After I left the club, I realized I didn't have my tennis racket with me, so I went back to get it. I saw a man, a good-looking man, I must say, holding it. I went over to him and said, 'You've got my racket.' He responded that yes, he did. And then he said that I could only get it back by giving him my name and phone number. Well I wanted my racket back, so I gave him my name and phone number. And that's how we met."

They all laughed together. There was silence for a while until Leslie asked Susan, "How did you meet your husband?"

Susan smiled and closed her eyes as if trying to remember every little moment of their early romance.

"Well," she said, "we met at a party. He was so good looking. He came over to me and he said, 'I'd love to take you out to dinner, would you come? Can I call you?' I said, 'Sure—call me sometime.' And then I gave him my phone number. He called me the next week and said, 'How about dinner tonight?' Well, I was free and thought I might like to go out with him. So, I said, 'Yes—I'd like that.'

He picked me up and we had a great dinner together. We seemed to have a lot in common. I knew I had a great time—I hoped he had, as well.

"He called me the next week, and we went out again. This went on for a couple of months. Then the calls grew less frequent. Or, he'd call me at the last minute, for instance, around six o'clock, and say, 'Hey kid, how about dinner tonight?' I didn't like that. He was beginning to take me for granted, and I didn't appreciate that. So, the next time he called me to ask me out, I told him, 'Sorry, I'm busy.' And he didn't like that. The next week he called me in the afternoon to ask, 'How about dinner tonight?' And I responded that I was busy that night—but thanked him for the invite. The next day he called me and said, 'I really want to see you. Can I come over, please?' And I said, 'Is there something you need to tell me?' And he said, 'Yes—there is. I want to talk to you about something.' 'Is it important?' I asked. And he said, 'Yes—it's very important. I'll be there at six o'clock.' And I said, 'Alright, I'll be here.'

"When he arrived, he pulled me into his arms and said, 'I really want to ask you something, it's very important to me.' So, he sat down and pulled out two diamond rings. 'I love you—I want to marry you—pick the diamond ring you like best.' So I looked at them and I couldn't decide which one of them I liked best. And he couldn't decide which one he liked best. So we kept both. And I wear them both sometimes and sometimes just one at a time."

Susan lifted her hands and showed everyone the diamond rings he had given her.

"What a beautiful story," Mildred said. "How romantic can you get?"

Pearl just sat there, looking at them. "I wish I had a story like that to tell. I met my husband when were in college. It was a romance that evolved from a friendship. And that was good, because it's good to be friends with your spouse."

The four women enjoyed each other's company. Leslie now felt very much a part of the Palm Beach Palace. She was enjoying the people and the activities. Resultantly, she rose. "Sorry girls—I've got to get to my exercise class. If I don't exercise and keep eating the desserts I've been eating, I'll turn into a flabby old lady. I've sure enjoyed spending time with you today. Maybe I will see you later at the show."

And she went off to the exercise class, which she took two mornings a week. She enjoyed the class more than she thought she might have. Some of the residents who were in the class had to sit to do their exercises, but the rest—including Leslie—were able to stand on their feet to follow the teacher's instructions. Some of the exercises required people to stand up and perhaps hold on with one hand to their chair. Some could, some couldn't. Leslie felt strong enough to be able to do the exercises without support.

She thought she would have a swim in the late afternoon and decided to rest a little in her apartment before dinner.

After dinner, many of the residents went into the spacious lobby where there were comfortable sofas and chairs, while others went up to their apartments. The bar was open; Leslie ordered a Manhattan. As she was sitting down with her drink, Norman came into the foyer and saw her. He came over and sat down beside her.

"Hi Les—how you doing?" he asked.

"I'm doing fine. How's your project going?" She asked him.

"Oh, I think we're in business. It's all set for tomorrow. I've had somebody on each floor put a little note under everyone's door saying we're going on strike tomorrow morning."

Leslie laughed. "Good luck with your project. I'll be down there to do whatever you may need." Then she asked, "Have you been happy here, Norman?"

"Oh, yes! After my wife died, I tried living alone. I love to travel, but I don't like to travel on my own. Someone told me about the Palm Beach Palace. I liked what I saw, and I've been pretty happy living here ever since." Norman said.

"Same here," said Leslie. "It's so nice to be able to talk to people of your own generation. We're lucky we have places like this. When I had to put my father into a nursing home, there was nothing like this around. They were so cold looking, and nothing was done to make them happy or interested in living. We're lucky to have a place like this."

"Yes, we are," said Norman. "Are you going to the show tomorrow night?"

"Well," Leslie said, "I guess I will, but I sure didn't like the last one I saw. The man was a dud. Well, he was okay, I guess."

Norman replied, "Every once in awhile you get a good performer. The one a few weeks ago wasn't as bad as some of the performers I've seen. He wasn't great, and sometimes you get lucky. But, you know the Palace doesn't pay a great fee to the performers. So, what do you expect—you get what you pay for."

"You're right—you get what you pay for. Maybe one of these weeks we'll be lucky and get a good one."

CHAPTER EIGHT

A Diamond in the Rough

And so it happened the next night, Leslie met Susan at the entrance to the auditorium, again. As usual, most of the seats were filled. They had a problem finding two together, but they finally spotted two seats in the fifth row. Again, many walkers were lining the walls of the theatre. People were waiting for the performance to start.

Then, a young man came out on stage. He was of average height. His hair was light brown, and so were his eyes. He seemed to be in his mid-twenties. He was a little nervous, and anxious for the audience to like him. He could have been the grandson of some of the people sitting there.

He announced to the audience, "I am so lucky to be here, folks. I am so happy that the Palm Beach Palace has allowed me to perform for you. I'm very young, but I think I have talent. But you people are the judges. You let me know what you think of my ability to perform. I would like to sing some songs for you, and I will know from your response what you think of me."

Leslie whispered to Susan, "Oh, another one of those."

As the young man started to sing, however, Leslie perked-up. She said to Susan, "He is good—he's very good."

After three songs, the performer said, "I didn't tell you my name. It's Gary. I live at home with my parents. I work full-time at a job that I don't like. And I want to be a performer. I want to be a singer. I want to please you, and I hope I have."

The audience burst into a round of thunderous applause. Gary grinned ear to ear. "Thank you, folks. It helps me a lot to know that you like me. Would you like me to continue singing?"

There was a great round of applause and cheers. "Okay," said Gary, "I'll sing some of my favorites." And he did.

When the performance was over, Leslie said to Susan, "I wonder if he has an agent."

Susan looked at Leslie. "What difference does it make to you? What do you care?"

"Well, I think he's just great. He has a job he doesn't like, plus he wants to be a singer. I think I might be able to help him."

"What do you know about that? This is show business." Susan replied.

Leslie said, "I used to work in an art gallery. That was art business and this is singing business. Business is business. I'm going to ask this Gary if he has an agent."

Several people had gone up to talk to Gary, and Leslie waited until they had left to approach him. She started, "I really enjoyed your performance. You're so much better than the other folks that they have performing here. Can I ask you a question?"

"Sure. What is it?"

"Do you have an agent?"

"No, I don't. I'd love to get into the business, but I have this full-time job. Sometimes I perform for free, but sometimes I get lucky and get a job like this here at the Palace. It doesn't pay much, but it gives me a bit extra and allows me to do what I love."

"Well, I wonder if you'd be interested in letting me represent you," asked Leslie.

Gary looked at her. "Are you an agent?" He asked.

"No, not really. But I know a lot about business— and business is business. So, if you don't mind giving me your full name and your phone number, I can try to see if I can book you at a bigger place than the Palm Beach Palace, which may start a new career for you."

"Well," answered Gary. "I don't think there's any harm in that if you think you can do something for me. Sure—here's my phone number. My full name is Gary Gordon. I am always home at dinnertime after I get home from work. If you have any success getting a show date, let me know."

Susan was waiting for Leslie in the rear of auditorium. "How did it go?" She asked.

Leslie was gleaming. "Oh, it went very well. I am going to be his representative. I think this guy is going to be a star some day. Maybe not a Sinatra, but I think he'll be able to quit his mundane day job, and do the singing that he loves so well. I am going to be his agent, and I am going to start on that tomorrow."

Susan said, "Come on, Leslie. What do you know about show business?"

"Business is business. I don't care if it's the shoe business or show business. I am going to go to one of the big hotels here and get Gary an audition. We'll see what he does before a real live paying audience."

"Well, good luck to you, Leslie," Susan said. "I think I am going up to bed."

"I'm going up to bed, too," said Leslie. "I feel really good about this. I cannot wait to get started tomorrow."

The next morning was the day of the strike that Norman had arranged. Leslie came down to breakfast and sat at the table with Susan, Mildred and Pearl. The waiter came over to take their order and they just sat there, not saying a word. The other residents came down to their tables and did the same thing. Nobody ordered anything—they just sat silently. Norman smiled with delight. His plan was going so well.

After an hour of just sitting, the director of the Palace came in and wondered why no one was eating. He said, "What's going on folks? Why aren't you ordering?" Nobody said a word.

Finally, Norman spoke up. "I'll tell you what's happening. We want things to stay the way they were. We want the waiters back. We want pancakes." Then everyone picked up their forks and shouted, "We want pancakes! We want pancakes!"

The director looked at Norman and said, "Is that what this is about? You folks won't order breakfast until you get pancakes?"

Norman replied, "It isn't just about pancakes. We hear that you're letting most of the waiters go. We hear it will be self-service. We don't like that. We pay good money to stay here, and we expect to get what was promised to us. We don't want to have to get our own breakfast. We want to be able to order what we were able to order before all of this came up. And we want it served to us. We will sit here until you promise to rescind this new staffing experiment, and give us our original breakfast privileges."

The director thought for a moment. Then he responded, "Okay—you win. The breakfast menu will stay the same as it always has been. And we will rehire all the waiters we let go. You will get the same service you always had."

Norman laughed. "Thank you. The service hasn't been that great, but it's been better than none at all. Okay folks, let's order breakfast." And they happily did.

Leslie went to the auditorium with Susan the following week, when Gary was scheduled to appear. As he entered the stage, everyone applauded before he even opened his mouth. He bowed, waved his hand at the audience, and said, "Thank you, dear people. What a pleasure it is to be here and to be greeted so warmly. I have selected a few songs that I love, and I want to sing them for you if you'll allow me." The audience all clapped warmly. Some even cheered.

After the performance was over, Leslie went up to him and said, "I have an appointment with the manager of the Florida Grand Hotel on Monday, and I'm going to tell him about you. Keep your fingers crossed that he will like what I have to say."

The following day, which was Sunday, Leslie met with Susan, Pearl and Mildred. Leslie told them that she was meeting the manager of the Florida Grand. Pearl looked at her, "You really think that you can pull this off?" she asked.

"Well, you never know, I just might get lucky enough to convince him to let Gary appear before an audience at the hotel," Leslie responded.

Susan laughed, "You sure have a lot of nerve, don't you Leslie?"

Leslie responded, "If you don't try, you'll never know. All he can do is say 'no' if he doesn't like the idea."

At her first opportunity, Leslie called to make an appointment with the public relations director of the Florida Grand. She explained that she was the manager of a talented young singer and wondered if he could perform on Saturday evening—just one song, at no charge. He could do it for free, just to get the public reaction. The social director was called to the conference, and they decided to give Gary a try. One song only would be allowed. They gave Leslie the booking date for Saturday evening two weeks away. Leslie went back to the Palace feeling as if she was walking on air. She called Gary, told him what she had done, and beamed with pleasure when she heard how thrilled he was.

"Do you have a tuxedo?" Leslie asked him.

"Me, have a tuxedo? Are you kidding? Where did I ever go? Where would I wear one?" Gary laughed.

"Well, then you better rent one. I'll pay for it. Now, the first thing you have to do is to decide what you're going to sing, and then you should have a second song ready, just in case."

"What do you mean, 'just in case'? In case of what?"

"Well, you never know, the audience might like you so much that they want a second song."

Gary laughed. "What an optimist you are. Okay, I'll pick out two songs."

"And Gary, you can try them out here at the Palace next Saturday, a week before you go on at the Florida Grand. I've spoken to the social director here and everything's a 'go.'"

CHAPTER NINE

Gary Makes a Plan

The next night was Leslie's evening to have dinner with Norman. After they had placed their orders, Norman said, "Leslie, what do you really know about that kid, Gary? You're getting involved with someone you don't know very much about. What's his background?"

"Well, it's true I don't know too much about him. I know he is very talented. He has been singing all his life around the house. He's good, but he needs direction. And that's what I'm hoping to give him."

"You realize you're getting yourself into a lot of work?"

"Sure, I know that, but that doesn't scare me. I've done my share of that, Norman. I just can't sit around all day without accomplishing anything. This will give me something exciting to do. Plus, I'll be helping this kid to create a better life for himself."

"He's got a family, doesn't he?" Norman asked.

"Sure he does. He lives with his parents, and he has a younger sister."

"So, why not just let his parents help him?"

Leslie laughed. "They've heard him singing around the house since he was a little kid. It's become a normal way of life—too familiar to them. I'm sure his parents advised him to get a job when he graduated school, get married, and then have kids. Most don't even think about a career like I hope Gary will have."

"Well, good luck, Leslie. You're going to need it."

"Thanks, Norman. I know I will."

The next evening at dinner, Leslie noticed that Betty had on a blonde wig. She was sure it was a wig, because it didn't fit her too well. Leslie asked, "Betty, are you blonde because you think blondes have more fun?"

Betty answered, "Some do. Some don't. I just wanted to give it a try."

Then Big Al spoke. "I hear you're going into show business, Leslie."

Leslie laughed. "Not exactly. I'm just trying to help a young kid who has a lot of talent and doesn't know how to use it."

Frank raised his wine glass. "Let's give a toast to Leslie and her protégé," he said.

And then they all raised their glasses and toasted, "Santé."

Then Frank said to Leslie, "It sounds like you're going to have a lot of fun—good for you. Good luck to you." And he raised his glass again to salute Leslie.

The next morning, the women busily questioned Leslie.

"You said if you got Gary booked into the Florida Grand, then maybe we could go. Can we, Leslie? Can we?"

"Yes, you can. I have arranged with the director to reserve a table down front."

Mildred said, "That's great. What are you going to wear, Leslie?"

"I don't know—I haven't thought about it. I think I will wear my black cocktail dress. It always looks good for these occasions," Leslie responded.

Mildred added, "I think I am going to buy a new dress—maybe a red one."

Pearl was silent, and then she perked-up. "There's a dress that I've been saving for a special occasion. Maybe this is that occasion."

Susan said, "I'll look over my wardrobe and decide a little later."

Leslie brightened up. "Maybe Frank will pour a special glass of wine for us tonight to honor Gary."

The week passed by quickly, and Saturday night was suddenly here.

The four women were excited. They were all dressed in their best clothes, and looked forward to a great evening. Leslie got them seated at their assigned table and went backstage. There was Gary in a rented tuxedo looking wonderful. He could have been a Hollywood star. He was in his element. He was going to be performing before an audience that had paid to hear him.

Leslie gave him a hug and said, "Break a leg, boy. I know you can do it." And then she went back to her friends. They all ordered drinks; Leslie had a margarita and her friends ordered wine. They all settled back to hear Gary perform.

The orchestra had been playing music suitable for dancing.

When the music stopped, the orchestra leader said, "I have a surprise for you. We have discovered a new talent. He will sing only one song, which he has chosen. I hope that you will like him. We do. His name is Gary Gordon and I think that you will hear more from him in the months to come. Come on out, Gary, we're all waiting to hear you."

Gary walked onto the stage, and bowed to the audience, as well as to the orchestra leader. He said, "It is an honor to be here with you folks. I would like to sing one of my favorite songs." The band began to play, and Gary started to sing. The room, which had before been noisy with people talking, fell silent. Everyone looked at him. Everyone listened intently.

When the song was over, the audience applauded wildly. Gary bowed, and started to walk off the stage. The orchestra leader called him back. He said, "Gary, they seemed to like you. How about singing another song?" Leslie couldn't believe it. The public relations person had said only one song and now Gary had been asked to sing another.

Gary looked at the orchestra leader and held up one finger. He said, "I was planning to sing just one song." The orchestra leader responded, "Never mind. They want you to sing another one." And Gary did.

When his performance was over, the orchestra leader said to Gary, "I think you have a great future in front of you. We'd love to have you back when we can arrange it."

The band began to play dance music again. Leslie excused herself from her friends, and went backstage to find Gary standing with a big smile on his face. You could tell how pleased he was, and of course, so was Leslie. She hugged him and said, "Gary, this is it. Your career is just starting. You were great! I am so proud of you."

The public relations man had been in the audience listening to Gary. He came backstage and shook Gary's hand. "You were great, Gary. I congratulate you. How would you like to appear at our downtown hotel in Miami Beach? I'm sure we can find a spot for you."

Leslie asked, "Will he be given a fee?"

The public relations man replied, "Of course. He's a talent. We will pay him $350.00 for the evening, plus expenses. How about it, Gary?"

Gary was bursting with pride. He said, "I would be very pleased to do that."

Leslie said to Gary, "I'll go with you, if you like. I can make things easier for you, if just for the one night. I have a feeling that you'll be leaving your daytime job very soon. I'll also get working on more performance dates for you. Get a good night's sleep, boy. You're going to need it." And she went back to her friends who were so excited to have witnessed the beginning of a new career for Gary Gordon.

The next day, Gary called his girlfriend, Ruth, to tell her the good news. "Oh, I'm so happy Gary. I'm so happy for you." She told him.

Gary said, "Ruth, I haven't seen you in a couple of days, how about dinner tonight?"

"I'd love that," she responded. When Gary went to pick Ruth up for their dinner date, she put her arms around him and gave him a big kiss. "I love you so much, Gary," she said.

Ruth was almost as tall as Gary. Her blonde shoulder-length hair was blowing in the gentle breeze. When she smiled, her dimples showed which made her even more perfect in Gary's eyes. She was not only pretty, but also slender.

That night at dinner, Gary told Ruth something that was weighing on his mind. "That woman, Leslie," he said, "is starting to drive me wild. She's been so good to me, but on the other hand, she makes all the decisions. She wants me to do this, and she wants me to do that. I don't know what to do about it. She insists that I get my own apartment, and she wants me to change my wardrobe.

"And when I told her about you, she told me that I shouldn't have a serious girlfriend. She thinks that I shouldn't be too involved with anyone just yet. I just don't know what to do about her."

They both sat in silence until Ruth pickedup her wine glass, raised it, and smiled at Gary. "I think I have an idea. My father has a friend who is a widower. He's not rich, but he has enough money to live a good life. And he's lonely. I wonder if he'd be interested in taking Leslie out a couple of times a week."

Gary looked at her. "What do you mean take her out a couple of times a week? What would that do for me?"

Ruth smiled. They both raised their glasses. "Don't you see what this will do? It will keep her so busy, she won't have time to bother you."

Gary laughed. "You are wonderful, Ruth. No wonder I love you so much."

They talked about their future, especially in light of Gary's recent success. He had given up his day job, and was currently taking special lessons to enhance his voice. The future was starting to look very good for both Gary and Ruth.

That night, when Ruth returned home, she sat down to talk to her father.

"Do you remember your friend, Donald?" she asked him.

"Sure I do. Why do you ask?" He responded.

"Well, I was wondering if he would be interested in meeting a lovely lady that Gary knows."

"What are you talking about?"

"I'm talking about introducing him to Leslie. She has done a great job with Gary, but she wants to control his life too much. He doesn't like that, and I don't like it either. If we could persuade Donald to date Leslie a few nights a week, then she'd have less time for Gary."

"Well, I'm not sure," replied Ruth's father. "But I can certainly ask him."

"I'd appreciate that, Dad," Ruth said. "Let's see what we can do to cut back her time with Gary."

"I'll give him a ring tomorrow. Maybe he will or maybe he won't. I'll give it a try."

The next day, Ruth's father called Donald. "There's a nice lady—she's a widow—who's been helping Gary with his vocal career. I was wondering if you'd like to meet her."

"Well, I certainly wouldn't mind meeting a nice lady. I haven't been doing much dating since Lillian died," Donald responded. "Sure. Why don't you give me her number, and I'll call her."

"No. I think it's better if we get her over here and then have you just casually drop in. Then we can introduce the two of you."

"Alright, I'll go along with that," responded Donald.

The next day, Leslie had set up an appointment to see Gary. While they were talking business, he said to her, "Leslie, there's a man I know—a very nice man—who's a widower. I told him about you, and he said he'd like to meet you. How about it?"

Leslie looked at him. Her eyes wide with wonder, "Well that's a surprise, Gary, as well as a bit of a switch. Here I've been managing you, and now you're going to manage me!" They both laughed.

"How about I bring him over here to the Palace and introduce you two? You can take it from there. You can go out on a date with him if you like. If you don't like, then you don't like. How would this Saturday work?"

"No," Leslie reminded Gary. "You can't do it Saturday. You have a date that night at the Imperial Hotel. Don't you remember?"

"Oh, I forgot about that," Gary responded. "Well, what about the following Friday?"

"Yeah, that's open. You can bring him over and we'll see what happens."

CHAPTER TEN

Girl Talk

The next day, Leslie was relaxing at the pool with her friends Susan, Mildred and Pearl. Leslie stood up and stretched her arms, almost touching the sky. It was a bright, sunny day. The pool looked so inviting. The palm trees trembled in the light breeze. It was a perfect day. She felt so good. Leslie said, "I'm beginning to put on weight. It's those desserts, I think. We never used to eat dessert after dinner every night—just for the occasional event. And now I order dessert every evening because everybody else does."

"I've been wondering, Leslie. What was your marriage like?" Pearl asked.

Leslie answered, "It was alright. Bruce was good, in his way."

"What do you mean 'in his way'?"

"Well, the usual, you know. He provided for the family and was a responsible husband."

"But did the two of you have any real challenges?"

"What do you mean?"

"Well, I mean, in your sex life, for example. Was it good?" Pearl asked.

"Well I don't know what you mean by asking if it was good. Bruce was the only man I ever had sex with. So I'm not sure if it was good, or otherwise. I wouldn't know what to compare it to."

"You mean you never had sex with any other men before Bruce?"

"That's right. I was a virgin when I met him, and I was a virgin when I married him. What was it like with you?" Leslie asked her.

"It was interesting. I did have sex before I was married."

"So you could make comparisons, one with the other?" Leslie asked her.

Pearl laughed. "Yes, I suppose I could make a few comparisons. But, you know something? I really didn't see any difference in the experiences."

The girls had a good laugh, and then they sat silent for a while.

Susan laughed, "What a strange subject we're talking about. What satisfies one might not satisfy another."

Leslie said, "My mother used to say that women really weren't interested in sex. She said that they didn't enjoy it. She said that men enjoy it much more, but not women."

"Oh, your poor mother! She didn't know what she was missing," said Pearl.

"I suppose that's true, Pearl." Leslie conceded. Then she turned toward Susan. "Oh Susan, I've been meaning to ask you a question. What's the story about Frank and the wine? Why does he have so much wine? Where does he get it all? Goodness! He brings a different bottle every night!"

"Well," Susan replied, "he was married to a very rich woman. When she died, he didn't want to stay in the house without her. He can't walk without help, and that's why he's got the scooter. He enjoys his nice wine and eating with other people. And that's why he brings a bottle every night. He buys it by the case, so he always has a good supply."

"I see. That makes sense. He's quite generous with it. He doesn't seem very friendly, though," Leslie commented.

"Oh, in his own way he's okay. I don't happen to like his manner. He became engaged to one of the women here, and then he dropped her like a hot potato. So watch it, Leslie. Just keep an eye out if he makes a move for you," Susan advised her with a coy smile.

The next evening, Gary had a gig at the Imperial and again, people were so enthralled by the way he sang that they immediately stopped their talking to simply sit and listen to him.

After the show, when Leslie went backstage to tell Gary how good he had been, she said, "I'm going to try to get you an interview with one of the leading TV hosts."

Gary was delighted. "That's great, Les. Hopefully that should lead to other opportunities in my career."

Leslie asked, "You remember the spot I got for you in that show in New York?"

"Yes," Gary responded.

"Well, the show has been confirmed, but I'm sorry to tell you that I won't be able to go with you."

Gary said, "Don't worry about it. I can certainly do it on my own. You've taught me so much already. But, tell me, how come you won't be able to make it?"

"Well," Leslie said, "I had a call from a man. You know the man who you brought to meet me at the Palace?"

"He called you, did he?"

"Yes he did. He called to ask if I would go out for dinner with him the night you are doing the show. I said that I had to be with you that night. He told me that you can do it on your own. He said, 'I know the boy, I know Gary well. He can do it, even if you're not there.' So I'm going to go out on this dinner date if you don't mind, Gary."

"Mind? Of course I don't mind. I'm delighted for you," Gary said excitedly.

The next day, when Gary told Ruth about his conversation with Leslie, they both laughed. It looked like this was going to work—it looked like they were going to be able to create their own life together, without Leslie trying to manage every detail and moment of Gary's life.

When Donald came to the Palace to take Leslie out, he commented on how nice the Palm Beach Palace looked. He especially liked the large foyer and its comfortable furniture. He pointed to the chandelier, and remarked on how attractive it was. "You certainly picked a nice place to retire in," he commented. "It looks lovely and you look lovely, too. We're going to one of my favorite restaurants," he continued. "I hope you like it as much as I do."

During dinner, he and Leslie found they had a lot in common. They both liked music, the theatre, and they both liked to travel, they both enjoyed meeting new friends and having new experiences. When he brought her back to the Palace and said goodnight, he asked if she would have dinner with him the following week. She quickly agreed.

They began to spend every Saturday night together and eventually every Wednesday evening as well.

Gary could not have been happier. He was spending less time with Leslie, and more and more time with Ruth. Gary wanted to reimburse Donald the money he was spending on dinners. He knew Donald was not rich, and he was doing Gary such a big favor by occupying Leslie, so that she had less time to spend with Gary. But Donald refused any pay. After all, he was enjoying his new relationship with Leslie and was doing it as much for himself as he was for his friend's son, Gary.

Gary's name was beginning to appear on page six of the New York Post and on the entertainment shows. He was doing more and more interviews, and he decided to get a talent manager. He needed arrangements for his songs, and was looking for new material—something Leslie could not do for him. Any other time she might have objected to Gary's search for a talent agent. Before she may have felt like an agent might infringe on her territory. In earlier days she would have stopped Gary from looking for someone else because she considered it her job. But now she was becoming more and more interested in Donald, and less enamored with being a business manager for Gary. It didn't matter to her that someone else might be coming in to do some of her duties—in fact, she even welcomed the idea.

Leslie arranged an appointment with Gary to discuss their evolving professional relationship. He came over to the Palace to talk with her.

"Gary, I'm sorry I've dedicating so little time to you. The days are flying by, and I'm spending more and more time with Donald. I'm afraid I'm not doing you justice."

"Leslie, how can you say that? You've done so much for me," Gary responded. "As a matter of fact, I didn't tell you that I've had an offer from Lloyd Price. That's not his real name of course—his real name is Paul Green. That's his show business name. Price has offered me a lot of money to sing with his band, exclusively. For a couple of nights a week, I'll make $5,000 dollars a show. All I have to do is get up on stage, and sing with his band."

Leslie got up and hugged Gary. She laughed and said, "I think you can give up your old day job, now." And then they both laughed.

Gary asked, "How about you, Leslie? How are things going with Donald? What's your relationship like?"

"Oh, I wouldn't call it a relationship. We seem to like each other. We seem to like the same things. I don't know where it will take us. I don't really care where it takes us because I feel this is a great friendship. I thank you for arranging the time to meet him. All I want from you, Gary, is the privilege to come to some of your concerts and the chance to bring Donald along."

"You got it, Leslie. Front row seats for the two of you," Gary said.

Leslie came down for breakfast the next day and sat down at a table with Susan.

Susan said, "Wow! You sure have a twinkle in your eye! What's up?"

Leslie responded, "I really don't know. I know that my life has changed since I came to the Palace.

I feel like I am starting anew all over again. Donald and I seem to be so well together. You know, Bruce was okay in his own way, but when I look back at our life together, I think it was a little on the dull side. He was a good husband, but when I'm with Donald, we laugh together; we have so much to say to one another. We even go dancing. I love that. Bruce never even called me 'honey,' or 'sweetheart,' or even 'dear.' But Donald does it all the time. I like that. Bruce never called me anything but 'Leslie,' And Donald always calls me 'honey.' I really like that."

Susan smiled, "You sound like you're falling in love again, Leslie."

"Oh I wouldn't say I'm falling in love. I just like the way Donald treats me. I love laughing with him. And now that I'm not managing Gary anymore, I have enough time to go out—day or night. We're taking it bit by bit; little by little. We'll see what the future holds. Thanks to the Palm Beach Palace, I now have a new life. I'll let you know what happens when I know what the future holds for me."

Susan smiled. "I'm so happy for you, Leslie. One never knows what tomorrow will bring."

CHAPTER ELEVEN

Another New Beginning

Gary was making a name for himself; he was appearing on television more frequently. And his name was in the entertainment section of newspapers. He was a celebrity now in his own right. Leslie was so proud. She had taken a hidden talent and made it a big one. Maybe she didn't know too much about show business, but she knew how to manage a business. And now she had a chance at creating a new life for herself if she chose to do it.

That night at dinner, Susan raised her wine glass and said to the group, "To Leslie. We don't know what her plans are for the future, but I think we should all say 'Santé Fe' to Leslie's new romance. Let's all say 'Santé Fe' to Leslie." And they all stood and said, "Santé Fe, Leslie. May your future be as bright as you are!"

Frank said, "We've always said, 'Santé,' but in this case, I'll go along with you, Susan. Santé Fé it is!"

Leslie took in her friends' well wishes, scanned the table and contemplated her life. She wasn't sure what path she would follow. She found she enjoyed the company of Donald and she knew she enjoyed being a talent agent. How many years lay ahead of her? No one knew. But she knew she wanted to enjoy her life from then on. She owed no one any obligations. She would take it day by day, year by year. She knew that whatever path she followed—whether it be the challenge of a career or the companionship of a man like Donald—she would savor it. There was a whole new world waiting for her. And she was sure she would enjoy whichever path she took.

She looked at her friends around the table and smiled. The future looked exciting to her and she was ready to face it.

The following day, Leslie had her usual date with Donald. When he came to take her out he was humming a tune. She stood and listened. He asked, "What are you listening to?"

"You! Donald, you really have a nice voice." Donald said, "Oh, I'm always humming around."

"No, I mean it," Leslie insisted. "Let me hear you sing." So he sang a few bars and she said, "Now that's a fine voice. Let me try to get you a spot at the Palace." Donald laughed.

"You want me to sing in front of all those people? You've got to be kidding! I'm not a singer."

"Oh, yes. Yes, you are!" Leslie argued. "Let me get you a spot at the Palace, and we'll take it from there." Donald laughed again. "I'm no singer, Leslie, but if you want to try, go ahead. Of course, you know you would be my talent manager."

"You bet your life I'll be your manager," Leslie agreed. "Maybe I can do for you what I did for Gary. But," she added, "Whether you're a singer or not, I really like you."

"And I like you, too, Leslie," replied Donald. "However this ends up I know we'll have fun together."

"We certainly will." Leslie agreed.

CLAUDETTE,
THE HAIRDRESSER

When I was living in Toronto, Ontario, I had a hairdresser named Claudette. Claudette became my friend. We took to each other almost immediately. When I first met her I realized that she was indeed a very interesting person. The day I had my first appointment with her to get my hair done her hair was dark with blue streaks. I did not comment on her appearance and we had a friendly conversation about her work and my work. Mostly we talked about her work, though. She told me about some of her clients and I told her a few stories about my work, which was producing shows in a downtown theater. She got all excited when she heard that.

The next time I saw her, her hair was blonde. I did not comment on that. After all, she was a hairdresser and she could do as she liked with her hair. She also experimented with clothes. She told me she would take an old evening gown and refashion it. Or, she'd take a day dress, cut off the sleeves and then turn it into an evening gown. Claudette was fun. I never knew what to expect when I went to her salon to get my hair done.

One day, she said that she had been asked to chair a contest of hairdressers. Contestants were attending from Paris to Toronto. They would be judged on their ability to style models' hair. She asked me if I would I help her get some publicity for the event. I knew a number of people in the media and said I would try to help her. The event turned out to be very successful. We got a lot of press and were covered by TV. Claudette was very happy with the results. Of course, I didn't charge her. She was my friend. I just loved seeing Claudette every week and seeing the change in her appearance on each visit. One week her hair was pink. Another week it might be blue. That was the fascinating thing about Claudette. You never knew what she would look like when you arrived. Her husband, who was tall and handsome with dark hair, took all this in with a grain of salt. He was used to Claudette's various appearances and the shop was doing very well financially because there were several other hairdressers employed there and business was good. I was lucky that I was the one who was able to get weekly appointments with Claudette, and I looked forward to them.

Another time she told me that a movie star was starting a new line of cosmetics. Claudette wanted to get a franchise for her area. Her husband did not want her to do that. It would cost a lot of money and he did not see the need to take such a gamble. After all, there were many lines of cosmetics and even though the movie star's name would be on the label, it was just another brand. But Claudette was determined to pursue the idea. She asked me if I would help her to get some publicity. When I had helped her before, she had been so pleased with the results. Now this would be a bigger thing. She would pay me and I would try to get as much publicity as I could. Not only that, the movie star would come to our city in person to talk about the new line of cosmetics. Well, I did like Claudette, but I did agree with her husband. He told me quietly that they were constantly arguing about her going ahead with the franchise. He said there were days when he could hardly talk to her. But she was going on with the program anyway.

The movie star's name was Dorothy Lamoure. I decided the best way to get the best publicity for launching a cosmetic line was to have a luncheon for the media. So I arranged a lunch menu and picked out a select few of the press whom I thought could help us the most.

On the day of the luncheon I decided to drive Dorothy Lamoure to the hotel where the lunch was to be held. At the appointed time, she came down looking as gorgeous as she did on the screen. She was wearing a coral dress and a matching turban, and over her dress she had flung a full-length fur coat. In those days we did wear those coats. I thought the fur was sable. She was stunning. She got into my car and as we drove she started to talk. She didn't talk about the cosmetic line, she talked about her work. She almost cried. She had made a number of films with Bing Crosby and Bob Hope. But now she wasn't getting any work at all. She sobbed, "They're both working and they're both older than I am. And I'm not getting any work anymore." I really felt sorry for her. She had been a star for so many years and she was still so beautiful. I don't really think she was a great actress, but when she sang as she did in the films, she had a pleasing voice. And when the three of them, Bob hope, Bing Crosby and herself starred in a film, it did well. All I could do was sympathize with her.

We arrived at the hotel and everyone was delighted to see her. The invited press was seated at the luncheon tables along with Claudette. After the lunch, Dorothy Lamoure spoke. She explained why she was putting out this new line of cosmetics. She said she had been studying the need for a line of health-type creams, lipsticks, mascaras— everything that women might want to use. She had been researching with experts in the field and hers would be the best and healthiest line on the market. The invited media seemed to be impressed with Miss Lamoure's talk. And we did get a lot of coverage both in the newspapers and television.

Claudette went forward in purchasing the franchise. By this time Claudette and her husband were hardly on speaking terms. Dorothy Lamoure's cosmetics did not go over so well with the public. Claudette lost a lot of money. She and her husband separated and her beauty shop closed.

I never saw Claudette after that, but I never forgot her. Every time I have a garment that I thought I wouldn't wear anymore, I thought of Claudette and wondered what she would do with it. I knew she would make an unusual garment that only Claudette could make and wear. And I wonder what color her hair is today.

THE TAXI DRIVER

Gordon Taylor was sitting at the wheel of his taxi. He looked at his watch. It was 10 minutes before 4:00. Since he had finished his shift, it was time to turn in the cab and go home. As he started to drive after the light changed, he noticed a woman standing on the curb. She had been waiting for the light to change and was going to cross the street but couldn't move. Gordon guessed she was about 5'3" or 5'4" and rather fat. But then he noticed that she wasn't fat at all, but thoroughly pregnant. She had shoulder length dark hair that was blowing around her face. She looked miserable and, obviously, in pain. She was wearing a thin coat and looked frigid as she tried to pull her coat over her body. But she was too pregnant to be able to close the coat.

Gordon was an ordinary man—pleasant when things went right and moody and self-deprecating when they didn't. He could see that this woman needed help, but really wanted to get home to his own wife and children. On one hand, here was a human being who needed help with nobody around her offering it. He had a lovely family at home – a wife and two darling children that he loved so much. Still, he couldn't ignore the plight of the woman on the curb, so he pulled his cab over in front of her and asked, "Where are you headed? To the hospital?" She nodded. "Well, get in the cab and I'll take you there." She lowered her eyes and said, "I have no money for a taxi."

"That's all right. Don't worry about the money." he answered. "I'll take you. It's not far. Just get in the cab." She couldn't open the car door, so he got out and helped her get in.

"Where's your family," he asked her? "Why are you all by yourself?"

She didn't answer him. He drove her to the emergency entrance of the hospital and helped her out of the cab and walked her to the admittance desk. The woman was in so much pain; she could barely stand up and seemed about ready to fall to the floor. Gordon steadied her while he spoke to the attendant, "Here, she's ready to deliver, I think. You better get her in right away."

The office rang for the nurse and she was lead away to the delivery room. Gordon started to leave and the desk clerk called him back. "I need a name. What's her name?"

"I don't know. I just drove her here." Gordon answered.

"Well, we need a name. We can't just admit her without a name. What's your name?"

"I'll give you my name, but I have nothing to do with this woman."

"Well, give us your name anyway," the secretary said.

So Gordon gave his name.

"And your address?"

He gave his address and said, "I hope the baby's ok and that the woman's ok. I was just trying to help her out, you know, do her a service by driving her here. Good-bye."

Her went back to his cab, dropped it off, and returned home. His two children were watching television. He went into the kitchen where his wife, Gloria, was preparing dinner. This was the best part of the day as far as Gordon was concerned. He and his wife loved their home, though modest, and their two children.

At the dinner table that night, Gordon told his family about the woman he had driven to the hospital, and how the clerk there had repeatedly asked him to leave his name—even though he was no relation or even friend of the nameless pregnant woman.

In fact, the admittance office seemed to treat Gordon as if he was the father. His family thought that was funny and laughed and laughed about it.

The rest of the week passed as it generally did with no problems, until the mail came at the end of the week. There was a bill from the hospital where Gordon had taken the woman—whose name he still did not know. The bill inside the envelope was for charges for delivering the baby and the use of special nurses. He showed the bill to his wife. "I don't understand this," he said. "Why in the world are they charging me?"

"I guess it's because you brought her in. You said they asked you for your name and address."

"Yes, they insisted that I do that. I was just doing a citizen's good deed by giving her a lift. I don't know her and don't know if I'd even recognize her if I saw her again."

The next day Gordon called the hospital and asked for the billing department. He explained the situation—how he was the cabdriver and had seen the woman cold and suffering. He told them he was just helping another human being by driving her to the hospital at no charge (because she had no money). The accountant listened to Gordon's story, and said, "We have to be paid. The woman tells us that you are her husband and that you will pay the bill. And that's why we sent you the bill."

"Oh, for goodness' sake! I'm married to another woman and we have two children. The patient is lying to you. You better find out who she is, as well as the man who got her pregnant. I'm not involved with her in any way. That will teach me a lesson for helping someone."

"Well, your name is the only name I have."

"I suppose the only thing for me to do is to take a DNA test to prove I'm not the father, Gordon said. "That is, unless you have a better suggestion."

"No, I don't have another idea of what to do. But we need payment for this case. The woman has left the hospital with her baby and we have no idea where she went."

There was silence for a moment. Then Gordon said, "Sometimes it's better to mind your own business. I thought we were supposed to help each other in this world. There I was on my way home after a day's work. I see someone in distress and go out of my way to help them. I take her to the hospital without charging her cab fare. And now you want to charge me for her hospital fee rather than charging the person who has left her on her own. Does that make any sense? No. I think the best thing to do is come in for a DNA test."

"That would get you off the hook," the billing clerk affirmed.

"I'll do that. Anything to get this thing off my back," replied Gordon determinedly.

Gordon was furious. When he returned home he told his wife that he was going to get a DNA test.

His wife turned to him. "Why are they involving you so much? You had nothing to do with her." And then she stared more intently, "Or did you?"

"Of course, not. I've never seen the woman before. I have no idea who she is, where she came from or what her name is. Furthermore, I have two beautiful children and don't need any more. I thank you for giving them to me." They calmed down and smiled at each other. Yes, they were a great family.

"At any rate, I'm going to the hospital and take the test to determine that I am definitely not the father of the baby."

The next day he went to the hospital and was prepared for the test. He spoke to the lab technician and said, "You guys must think I'm running around the city making dozens of women pregnant. Believe me, I've got two great kids and it's all I can do to make enough money driving a cab to support them, give them a good home and provide them with all their needs, and hopefully make enough to send them to college when they grow up. I don't need any more kids. I've got two of the best already. That's all I want."

He waited after the DNA test to get the results, but they said it would take a few days and they'd call him. Gordon went home after he turned in his cab for the day, and had a rousing time playing with the children. After they put the children to bed, he and his wife had a good laugh about how the test would prove he was not the father of the unknown woman's child.

Two days later he was called by the hospital. They found that indeed he was not the father of the strange woman's child. They found that he was infertile and could not have children.

"What do you mean that I can't have children, he asked? "I have two children already!"

"Well, miracles happen. I don't know how you did it, but according to our tests, you can't conceive children." Gordon was so perplexed and upset by the test results that he turned in his taxi early and went home. The children were still in school. His wife came in. She had been out shopping for groceries. She noticed that Gordon was home much earlier than usual. "Taking a day off?" she asked pleasantly. "Sort of," Gordon answered. "I'm a little concerned about something."

"What is it, Dear?" she asked?

"Well, I can't quite figure this out. We have two adorable children, but my DNA test showed that I'm infertile and unable to have children."

Gloria's face reddened. "Well, they must have made a mistake," she said. "I have a friend who thought she was pregnant. Turned out that she wasn't. She was just eating a lot of ice-cream and got fat."

Gordon stood up. He was getting a little frustrated at this point. "Look. What I'm talking about is no light matter. If the hospital is right—and they assured me that they are—how is it that we have two children when I'm unable to have children?"

Gloria was silent and then she spoke in a low voice. "I wanted children so badly and we didn't seem to be able to conceive. Do you remember when we were on a cruise with our friends, Susan and Jake?"

"Yes, I remember the cruise," Gordon answered.

"Well, at one of the ports. I don't remember which one. You went off on a guided tour. Susan did too. I wasn't too interested so I stayed on the ship and so did Dick. We got to talking. We liked each other, but there was never anything between us. I told him we were trying to have a child, but that we couldn't have any. Dick thought about it for a while and said, "Well, maybe I can help." So I let him. It wasn't a real affair. He was able to make me pregnant and of course, you and I made love a couple of times a week, so there was no problem in your thinking that it was your child. It was your child in every sense of the word."

Gordon looked at her. He couldn't believe it. But he had to or he'd go mad. Then he said, "Well, now I understand what you're saying. But, what about the second pregnancy?"

"It was the same thing when we were on a different trip with them. There was another time we were alone. We never did it after that. You and I are lucky to have these adorable children. I feel guilty sometimes. But in a way, I'm glad I did it because of the family that we are now."

Gloria sat down. She began to rub her eyes. Tears began to well up and run down her cheeks. She didn't say anything. She just sat there. Finally, she looked up at Gordon who was standing over her.

"I wanted children so badly," she said, "and it didn't look like you could help me have them. I waited and waited, hoping a miracle would happen and nothing did. I wanted children. So I did what I did. I didn't mean to deceive you and you can divorce me if you want to. But I'm going to take my children with me if we split up. Gordon walked over to the window and looked out. His children were coming home from school. He could see them walking down the street toward their home. He loved them. He could not give them up. It was not his wife's fault that he could not give her children. It was his fault. He turned back toward Gloria and put his arms around her."

Gordon reached down and took her hand in his, "I understand why you did what you did. I don't like it, but I accept it, because if you hadn't done that, we wouldn't have the family that we have now."

When the children came in, Gordon turned to Gloria and gave her a big hug. It was a miracle to him that they had the family that they had. He had a fine home. He had two adorable children. He had a wife who did everything she could to make his life pleasant. What if he had not helped that poor unknown woman? He would have never known the truth. He had a good wife and said, "Let's all go out to dinner tonight and celebrate our family. I love you all."

And they did. After that Gordon never received another bill from the hospital. And he went straight home after work every day.

"Build Me A Pyramid!"

Three women were sitting in a hotel lobby waiting for their friend to join them for lunch. One of them, a fun-loving, fifty-something, blonde named Brenda, nervously looked at her watch and broke the silence. "I wonder why Lorraine's so late? She knows we have lunch every Wednesday and she's always on time."

The others murmured and assured her that she would be there any minute. Finally, Lorraine arrived at the hotel and went over to join her friends. They could see that she looked very unhappy. In fact, one of them whispered to the others, "It looks as though she's been crying!"

They got up, went into the dining room, sat down and ordered their lunch. They all looked at Lorraine. Brenda spoke first. "Is there anything wrong? What's the matter Lorraine?"

Lorraine's shoulder length auburn hair almost reached her shoulders. She was a real beauty. She tossed her hair and said, "I have something to tell you girls." She dabbed her eyes which were filling with tears. Her three friends leaned forward to catch every word Lorraine was going to say.

"I just came from the doctor," she said. "He told me that he received the X-rays and they showed that I have leukemia." Lorraine's friends gasped. "Oh no!" said Brenda. "Oh, you poor thing," said Pearl. Pearl was a good name for her. She always wore pearls. Pearls around her neck, and on her ears. She always wore something light grey that looked like a pair of pearls. Dorothy, a long-time friend, just looked at Lorraine, grabbed her hand, and said, "They got it all wrong, you know." "No," said Lorraine, "I saw the X-rays. And my doctor is a good one. He wouldn't have told me that if it wasn't true."

Lorraine was a very pretty young woman. She didn't like telling her age, but her friends knew she was forty-two years old. She had a slender figure and did not look her age at all. She had a career as a PR professional and never worried about making a living for herself. She had many proposals of marriage and decided not to marry but to carry on with her career. She was always in high demand with her work and enjoyed doing it. She also enjoyed the company of her friends and all three women at the table were her very best friends.

Lorraine was wearing a pale, grey jacket and her tears were flowing down her cheeks dropping onto the jacket. She reached for her handkerchief and tried to wipe the tears away.

Dorothy just sat there stunned and reached for Lorraine's hand. She said, "I don't believe that story, Lorraine. I want you to live forever." Lorraine sighed and said, "I'm afraid I can't manage that, but I would like to be around a little longer than six months."

Pearl sat with her elbows on the table. She leaned back in her chair and said, "Let's take this slowly Lorraine. You are one of us. The four of us have been through a lot together. You know you can count on us for anything that happens – good or bad. Now tell us slowly exactly what happened."

"Well," said Lorraine, "I've been seeing this doctor for quite a while because I had a little pain and he's been treating me. And now he says he can't treat me anymore. Someday, they'll be able to cure what I have, but that day hasn't come yet."

The waiter appeared with their food and they started to eat slowly. After hearing Lorraine's story, none of them were hungry. Nobody wanted to eat. They all finally gave up. Lorraine said, "I'm going to order cocktails for all of us because this might be our last lunch together." "For God's sake," said Pearl, "don't be so morbid. We're going to do everything we can to help you. The four of us have been friends since high school. We've all gone our separate ways in our careers. You have been very good at your work and there's no reason for you to stop it. As long as you have your energy, I want us all to hold hands and say a little prayer."

And they did. They sat at the table holding hands and drinking their cocktails. They also reminisced about some of the things they had done together. Two of the women were married, the third was dating a man who didn't seem quite ready to propose marriage. Lorraine looked around at her friends and thought how lucky she was to have friends like these.

They decided to go back to Lorraine's apartment and talk about things they had done, as well as things they would do over again if they could. Things they would always do together. The four of them vowed to remain friends forever.

Lorraine started to tell them about what she thought would happen and how it would happen. She said, "When I die, I want to be buried in a pyramid." They all looked at her. Pearl said, "You're joking!" Lorraine said, "No, I'm not. I just don't want an ordinary burial. I want to be buried in a pyramid." The three of them looked at each other and thought Lorraine was going mad. Pearl asked, "Where would this pyramid be?" Lorraine said, "I don't know. I'm going to look for some place that I think would be the right place for me and then I will hire an architect to build me a pyramid there." The three women laughed. "You're joking," Brenda said. "No, I'm not," said Lorraine, "I'm not joking at all. I've had a good life. I've had a good job. I never married, but I never wanted to. I've had a lot of proposals in my day, but I've enjoyed my work. I liked living alone after my parents died, so I found this apartment and fixed it up as I liked. I'm going to stay here as long as I can, but will plan my funeral the way I want to."

The three women nodded. Dorothy said, "OK Lorraine, it's your funeral. We'll go along with that. But believe me, I think your doctor might be mistaken and you might be the one outliving all of us."

Lorraine leaned forward, and said, "Here's what I've been thinking girls. I'm going to go out in the country and look for a place where I can build a pyramid. It's got to be the right place and I know I have at least 6 months to figure things out. I'm going to keep my job as long as I can. I make good money and if I have to, I will hire an architect to build me this pyramid." "OK," said Pearl. "How about we go around with you to find the right place?" Lorraine looked up and smiled. "Oh that would be fun. I would love it if you came with me." So they planned to go to find a place to build a pyramid for Lorraine and decided to go the following week. They went the next Saturday and drove into the countryside. "What did you have in mind Lorraine?" asked Brenda. "Well, I don't want too much sunshine and I certainly don't want a cold place. I want to be cozy and warm." "Would you like to be near the water?" asked Dorothy.

"Well, I don't mind being near the water if it's quiet. I don't mind if it has ripples and I don't want the water to come on the land. But I don't mind being near the water." "Alright," said Dorothy, "we'll go into the countryside near the lake and we can pick a spot that you think you'd like." So that's what they did. They drove out into the country, got out of the car, and walked around to see what Lorraine thought of this part of land.

Pearl smiled and said, "Here's a nice spot Lorraine! It has nice grass under the tree nearby that would keep you cool in the summer. It will be warm in the winter anyway in the coffin." "No," said Lorraine, "I don't like this spot. Let's move on."

"I think maybe the other side of the lake would be better because it would have the morning sun. It faces east and you know I just love lying in the sun." Pearl tried hard not to laugh. It seemed very strange to her. But Lorraine was trying to arrange her own funeral even to the extent of when the sun would shine on her. As though it mattered, since she would be in the coffin.

But if this pleased Lorraine, this arrangement of her own funeral, then they would go along with it. They spent the afternoon looking for the right site. And finally found it. It was beside a small lake. It had a tree with hanging boughs and it seemed like the perfect place to picnic or spend an afternoon. Or be buried there. But no one wanted to think about that part of it.

After all, why shouldn't Lorraine select the exact spot where she would be after she died? Why would she have to be in the cemetery with hundreds of other bodies around her? She had always been one to choose things for herself and never wanted to be in a crowd. Lorraine had always known what she wanted and if this was it, then this was what she would have.

The four of them sat down on the ground and felt very comfortable under the tree. Lorraine said,

"Yes, this is the right site for me. Thank you girls, for helping me choose where I want to be forever."

They went back to Lorraine's apartment and she brought out some wine, cheese and crackers. The four of them began to reminisce about some of the adventures they had as a group. They had all been friends since high school. Two of them had gone away to college. Pearl had found a position with a manufacturing company making housewares and was now VP of the company.

Lorraine reminded them of a time they had gone on a cruise where she had won two hundred dollars playing the slot machines. Pearl told them about the romance she almost had on that same cruise with the captain of the ship. Almost, but not quite. They had travelled together many times and remained close friends over a twenty year period.

None of them had married but two of them had come close to it. They all knew they had a rare friendship and enjoyed it. Everyone looked at Lorraine and thought, "She can't die so young! It's impossible." She was closer to them than if she had been a sister or a cousin.

They decided they would stay close by and make her feel great. If she was going to die, then they would be with her every second until that doomed day came. Settling back in her chair, Brenda asked, "So, who is going to make you a pyramid?"

"It has to be built, I guess. I don't know," said Lorraine. "I suppose I have to hire an architect." Lorraine sat up in her chair and said, "You know, I haven't thought through any of the details. I have to find an architect. Do any of you know any architects?"

Brenda spoke up. "My brother's best friend is an architect. My brother thinks he's a very good one. He built the plaza downtown, you know." "That's a great place," said Lorraine. "I always thought it was designed beautifully and I enjoyed going there."

Brenda chimed in. "Why don't I ask my brother to get this architect to call you?" "Okay," said Lorraine, "Done deal."

"I'll speak to him to see if he has any ideas." Her friends stood up. It was time to go home and let Lorraine rest. They would continue their great friendship with her and be available for her whenever she needed them.

When they left, Lorraine took out a sketch pad and started to draw a pyramid she had in mind. She had been thinking about it for some time and now was the time to accomplish what she had in mind.

She felt so much better having shared her thoughts with her three best friends.

She was now free to tell them what she had in mind. She knew that if she needed anything, she could always call on her friends. They had been so much a part of her life for so many years and she knew they would always be there for her.

She glanced about her apartment. It was tidy and suited her to a "t." Her bookshelves were filled with books she had enjoyed reading. She would read more if she had the time. She was not a great cook but then who would she be cooking for anyway?

Just herself. She loved her job. She enjoyed shopping for her clothes which were always in fashion, but not in a faddish way. They were always on the tailored side. Lorraine did not like fads.

She had never married although she could have. She liked her life the way it was. But not the way it was now that she had been given the bad news by her doctor.

The next day, she had a phone call from an architect. He told her his name and that Brenda's brother had asked him to call her. What did she want to tell him about?

Lorraine said, "I want to discuss this with you, but not on the phone. Could you come over sometime this week and we can go over what it is that I want?" They set up an appointment for the next evening and the architect, whose name was Richard Stone, knocked at her door at the agreed upon time. He was a tall man, well dressed with dark brown hair. His shoes were polished to a shine. His hair was combed neatly around his ears. She liked what she saw. Lorraine invited him in. He looked around the apartment. "Nice place you have here," he said. "Thank you," said Lorraine. "I enjoy it." "I don't live too far from here," he said. "My apartment is not quite as nice as yours."

"Well," said Lorraine, "I always try to make my surroundings important to me. And that's why you're here. If I can live the way I want, I want to die the way I want." He looked startled. "What are you talking about?" he said. Lorraine laughed. "I just don't want to be put in a cemetery with a hundred other people. I want a nice place for my coffin."

"I want nice surroundings. And I want to be buried in a pyramid." He looked at her. "You want to be buried in a pyramid?" She nodded. "Well," he said, "that's an unusual request." He never heard of anything like that before. "Well, now you have it," said Lorraine.

"That's what I want. And I want you to build me a pyramid." He leaned back and stretched his legs out. "Ah," he said. "You want a pyramid. I guess I could build you a pyramid. Where do you think you want it?"

Lorraine told him about her outing with her friends. "I think I've found the perfect place," she said. "I can show it to you if you want." "Sure," he said, "I'd have to see it. But do you know what you're doing? Do you really want to be buried in a pyramid?" Lorraine nodded her head in acknowledgement. "I certainly DO know what I want. And that's what I want. A pyramid."

"Alright, I'll build one for you. Why don't we drive out next Sunday to see the place that you have selected??

And so they did. He shook his head when he saw the place and said, "We can't possibly build a pyramid here. The county will not allow it. I think I know a place better suited for your pyramid. Why don't we drive out to see it next weekend"

The following week they did drive out to his suggested place, but she did not like it.

They spent the next few months together looking at various locations.

Each time they went out they got to know each other better, and found that they were becoming close friends.

After six months had passed, while they were driving out to yet another location, he looked at her said, "I have a suggestion for you. We've been to many location sites that I liked, and you didn't, and some that you liked and I didn't. My suggestion is to go to the real site. Let's go to the pyramids in Egypt."

She looked at him and her eyes grew wide. He put his arm around her. He said, "We started out as client and architect. We became friends. And I found myself more than a friend. I fell in love with you. Six months have passed and you've become more beautiful in my eyes. I'll take a chance on that six months deal. I'll keep you alive for the next twenty years, as long as we can be together, I'll take a chance on your being alive. I would like to take you to the real pyramids in Egypt. Will you come with me and make it a real honeymoon?"

She smiles. "I was hoping you would ask me. I'll go any place with you. I know wherever you go that will be the right location for me. You make me feel healthy and happy to be alive!"

He put his arms around her and kissed her and together they planned their trip to Egypt to see the pyramids.

SOUL MATES

Dennis had been waiting for the girls for some time. They should have arrived ten minutes ago. Something must have happened. Finally, they came. "You are late," Dennis said.

"Well," one of the girls said, "We had an accident."

"I know you did," said Dennis. "It was planned."

"You mean the accident was planned?" asked the other girl.

"Of course, it was," replied Dennis. "It was planned some time ago." The girls looked at each other. "You mean somebody planned the accident we just had?"

"Yes," said Dennis. "It was planned because we need you."

"Who needs us?" asked one girl.

"You'll see. Come with me." The girls started to follow him and began to laugh. Dennis was three feet tall. One of the girls looked at the other and said, "You are three feet tall, too." She looked at herself and saw that she was, too. They looked at each other and looked very confused. How had they lost all that height? How had they shrunk to three feet tall?

Dennis saw how confused they were, and said, "These are your souls. Everyone here is three feet tall. Your soul is now revealed to the world. We're on our way to arrange your future." They followed him into a large courtyard. There were many souls sitting around. No seemed to be taller than three feet. The girls looked at Dennis and one of them said, "What is this place? Who are these people? Why is everyone so short?"

Dennis replied, "You're in Soul Heaven. When you die on earth your soul comes here and those people who have lived a good life are entitled to live in this part of Soul Heaven."

"And where do the others go?" asked the girl.

"Now that's a good question. There's another part of Soul Heaven, but you don't need to know where that is. This is where you'll be and you may be able to make good friends with any of the souls you encounter."

The girls looked at each other and Mary Lou said, "I know who I want to meet."

"And I do, too," her sister said. "I'd like to meet Shakespeare."

Dennis laughed. "Everyone wants to meet Shakespeare when they come here. He's still very, very popular. But you'll have time to meet a lot of people. First you have to arrange your own souls and prepare yourself for the life you will be leading from now on.

"Can I ask you a question, Dennis?" asked Francine. "Is this life here an eternity? Will we live here forever?"

"I really don't know," replied Dennis. "I've been here for two hundred years and there certainly was life here when I came. We just do what we have to do and enjoy our time here. Now come with me and I will show you where you will be staying and the work that you will be doing."

He urged them on and pointed up where the clouds were, but two of them were empty. Just plain blank. The girls looked up at the empty clouds and looked back at Dennis.

"What are we looking at, Dennis?" she asked. "I see two empty clouds and the other clouds are all fluffy and white."

"That's exactly the point," said Dennis. "That's the job you've been assigned to. Mary Lou you will have Cloud 8 and Francine, you will have Cloud 9."

"What will we do with the clouds?" asked Francine.

"You will make them fluffy. You will make them white. It's up to you what you want to do with the clouds. But they must be beautiful. You will be given tools to make them full or make them dark. You can make it rain on the earth people down below."

"That doesn't seem like a big job to me," said Francine.

"You'd be surprised." Dennis replied. "It can be big job. Clouds don't always work together. Your cloud may be next to one that is rather ugly. You want yours to be beautiful. Now, that's up to you. You can create strokes. You can make a lovely pattern on your cloud. It's your choice. I do suggest that you two girls work together because you're artistic and you want to provide a lovely sight for the earth people down below.

"How many hours do we work in a day?" Mary Lou asked.

"Oh, maybe six to eight hours."

"Do we get time off?" She asked

"Yes, you do. And that's the time you'll be able to mingle with the other souls here and meet the people you liked down on earth."

"Where do we sleep?"

"You don't." said Dennis. "Souls don't require sleep. You can stroll along on your time off. You'll find things to do. It's up to you.

As they ambled, they saw Einstein talking to Steve Jobs. They saw Mozart talking to George and Ira Gershwin. While everyone in the room was chatting, there was no noise. Everything seemed so peaceful. Everyone seemed so content. Their souls were bared. Most of the people appeared very happy.

Dennis led the girls into another room. He said, "If there's anyone you want to contact who has left the other world you just came from, you can find them. There is a huge wall that has the names of almost everybody who has lead a good life in the real world. The names are arranged in alphabetical order."

He turned to the girls and said, "Now I will take you to your first assignment."

He turned to one of the girls, "Francine, here's Cloud 8. And Mary Lou, this is Cloud 9." The girls looked at Dennis, "You mean we'll really be working on clouds?"

"Yes," said Dennis. "You'll be working on clouds for a while until we assess your working habits. You mingle with other clouds or you can go your lone way. Of course you must consider what the weather is down on earth. You can't have puffy white clouds in the middle of icy January.

Up here in our world the weather is always nice. Down there, though in the other world, it sometimes gets very frosty or rains heavily.

So, you must remember that you can't have sunny skies and puffy clouds on those days."

"How long will we be on the clouds?" asked Francine.

"That depends on your work. The clouds will be your first assignment. If you pass that test, you will be assigned to something more important."

"What would that be?" asked Francine.

"I can't tell you now. We will assess your ability while you work on this first assignment."

"Where will we be living?" asked one of the girls.

"Living?" Dennis laughed. "Souls have a long life. They don't require food or sleep. Souls require honesty and truthfulness. Do your job properly and you can meet almost anybody who has come up to our heaven.

Now, I have another appointment. I must leave you to do your best. Good luck to you."

Then he disappeared to meet a new guest who had just come up to this other world—a good world where peace and harmony are taken for granted.

"Let's see what happens, Mary Lou said. "I'll get to work on Cloud 8, you work on your Cloud 9."

So they jumped into their clouds and got to work. Then they combined the two clouds together to see if it would make a thunder sound. But it didn't. The two clouds embraced each other and looked like huge marshmallows.

"This is fun!" said Francine. "I'm going to make a drawing on my cloud."

"Well, maybe I will too," said Mary Lou. So they each tried to out-do each other. One of them noticed a little curtain at the top of the cloud with a name at the bottom of the curtain. She pulled it down and the cloud vanished from her eyes. "Well of course. This is where the clouds go when you don't see them anymore. I wonder when we can step out of the cloud and reach some of the other souls who are out here."

"Let's ask Dennis," the other one said. There was a little bell at the bottom of each cloud. They rang one bell and Dennis answered, "Yes?"

"We were wondering how long we have to stay in the cloud."

"You will each be in the cloud for at least a week, and then we'll tell you more."

"How about our bed? When will we go to sleep?"

"Souls don't require sleep or food. They do require good thoughts and a good and pure conscience. You will put in at least one week on each cloud you are assigned to and then we will let you know where you go from there. If there is anyone special you want to meet, you will find a request form at the bottom of your uniform."

Mary Lou brought her cloud very close to Cloud 9. She asked Francine, "Would you mind very much if I tried to find your husband? He was such a good man. He must be up here now since he died five years ago." Francine laughed. "Do you really mean that? Did you really like him that much?"

Mary Lou said, "I really did envy you for being married to a guy like Joe. I always wished I could meet somebody like that. But it never happened."

Francine laughed, "If I had known that, you could have had him sooner. He certainly wasn't my idea of what a good husband should be."

"Well, what do you think a good husband should be like?" asked Mary Lou.

Francine said, "I think a good husband is a good husband, but also a good friend—someone who's a comrade. Someone you can talk to. Someone you want to tell things to and who will listen to you.

Someone with whom you can share your life until the day you die."

"And Joe wasn't like that?" asked Mary Lou.

"Not at all," said Francine, "Not at all."

"Well then, you don't mind if I try to find him, do you?"

"No, I sure don't. Good luck to you," said Francine.

So when it was time to pull the curtain over the clouds, Mary Lou set off to find Joe. She went to the great wall where all the names were listed alphabetically and looked to see where Joe might be. She found his name set out and discovered him with a group of other male souls. Joe was telling them a story. Mary Lou listened quietly as he related a tale he was making up as he spoke. And then he spotted her. "Well, well," he said. "Look who's here. Did you come up her alone or with my wife?"

Mary Lou said, "We came together. We had an accident. I wanted to talk to you. You probably don't know, but I've always wanted to talk to you."

"No I didn't know that," said Joe. "I had no idea that you ever gave me a second thought."

"Well, I couldn't make it obvious. After all, you were married to my sister."

"Yes," said Joe. "I was married to your sister. But she really didn't think she was married to me. She didn't try to be a wife. Unfortunately, after a while we just stopped caring for each other. But, tell me, when did you arrive up here?"

"Well, I don't know how you count days here, but it seems like a day ago. We are working our way on a cloud assignment," replied Mary Lou.

"Now, that's a good assignment," said Joe. "I'll look forward to sharing a really great friendship with you now and getting to know you. But, for the moment I must go back to my work. I'll see you later."

Mary Lou went back to her cloud and told her sister. "I found Joe." Francine laughed. "Good luck to you. I hope you have a good relationship with him—a better one than I did. Now, I'm going to take a little rest." Next, she pulled her curtain down halfway over Cloud 9. Mary Lou did the same with her cloud 8 and the world below them turned into dusk, and night began to make the world below dark. And all the clouds took a rest until the next day arrived.

The next day, they raised the curtains on the clouds and got to work. It was fun. They could make the sky sunny or dark, misty or clear. They felt so relaxed. Mary Lou said, "This cloud heaven is a great place. I'm so glad we were allowed up here. From what I can see, no one gets sick, no one grows tired. Everyone seems happy. Why don't we step out of the clouds and just walk around a little bit, see who's here, make some friends. Francine broke in, "We never asked Dennis about food. Where do we eat?"

"Oh," said Mary Lou. "That's right. But I'm not hungry. Are you?"

"No, not really," said Francine. "I can't remember the last meal I had, but I'm not hungry at all."

So the two sisters stepped out of their clouds and began to investigate their new world. They spotted a group of souls standing around a counter. They had glasses in their hands and were drinking some kind of liquid that looked like chocolate.

Francine said, "Let's go over there and see what they're drinking."

So the two souls walked over and saw a soul behind the counter. It was a male soul who had curly hair and a little mustache. He looked at the girls and said, "Want a drink, girls?"

"Sure," said Francine. "What've you got?"

"Anything you want. You just name it and I'll give it to you."

So Francine chose a chocolate soda and Mary Lou asked for water.

"Here you are, girls," said the bar-tender. "Enjoy your beverage."

The girls took their drinks and started to walk around Soul Heaven. Mary Lou turned to Francine, "Would you mind if I go visit Joe, again? "No," said Francine. "I'll just go along and see what this is all about. Just imagine, this is a world where everyone is happy. No one gets sick.

"I think this may be a great place for us," said Francine. "You go and visit Joe again and I'll take my time and look around. We can compare notes later when we return to our clouds."

So, Mary Lou went off to see Joe and Francine walked on. She walked over to a group of souls who were sitting in a circle. One soul was talking about something he had done on earth. He had been a scientist and collaborated with a group of people who were working on a nuclear bomb project. Although he did his job as well as he could, he was hoping that the project would be unsuccessful. "Who wants to blow up the world?" he asked the other souls. "Believe me, I did my best on the job. But I'm glad to be away from them. Wars! Who wants wars? Where do they get you? It just kills people and doesn't solve anything."

Francine nodded. Then she said, "You are so right. My sister and I just arrived yesterday in Soul Heaven and I think this turned out to be a great place for us. Peace. That's what we need."

The other souls looked up at her and applauded. "That's right. Peace on earth. Our group is working on that. That's our project."

"I have some time to spare. I only worked 6 hours a day on our cloud project. Can I join you?" Francine asked.

"Sure, we need all the help we can get." One of the souls spoke up. "There just seems to be no peace in some of the countries in Asia. Would you be interested in working in that area?"

"Yes, I would do that," She answered. "Anyplace I'm needed. I want everyone down there on earth to be safe and to be healthy, to have a good place to live and enough food to eat. Sure, I'll do whatever is necessary—whatever I can do to help."

She sat down and joined the group of souls and felt very much at home with them.

Mary Lou was on her quest to find Joe. But she couldn't find him anywhere. She saw a cluster of people listening to Shakespeare. Mary Lou had done some writing while she was on earth and had always loved reading Shakespeare's plays and sonnets. And here the renowned author was, surrounded by a number of souls—including Joe! Mary Lou joined them.

Mary Lou was very content listening to Shakespeare with Joe and very happy in her new home.

Printed in the United States
By Bookmasters